A HOME IN THE MIST I

A CADES COVE STORY

THE STRANGER

W.T. RIDENOUR

A HOME IN THE MIST I

A Cades Cove Story

THE STRANGER

W. T. Ridenour

To Kathy

Table Of Contents

Introduction

I N THE GREAT SMOKY MOUNTAINS of Eastern Tennessee, tucked away among rolling hills and picturesque peaks, lies a gently flowing valley that just may be the reigning jewel of the Appalachian range. Abounding with clear-flowing brooks, great expanses of windblown grasslands, and magnificent stands of both towering pines and majestic hardwoods, it's a land flush with natural wonders.

Scented by the blossoms of ever-present rhododendrons and mountain laurels, it's the ancestral home of deer, wolves, buffalo, and bears, along with a seemingly endless diversity of animals, both predator and prey.

Its vegetation and birdlife alone would rival any region on the planet.

Native Americans of countless tribes and bands

hunted this land of plenty for thousands of years before the first Europeans plowed the soil and built a settlement for their weary families. Then, in 1927, the U.S. Parks Department chose to make it part of the Great Smoky Mountains National Park.

This is the story of a few fortunate families, both red and white, who called this wonderland home. Who scratched out a living in the fertile soil of a mountain cove named after Chief Kade of the Tsiya'hi village. Who learned to rely on, and help their neighbors in equal measure.

This is America's story.

The author hopes you enjoy these mountain tales, and he encourages the reader to visit the site of their inspiration.

Prologue

AS IS OUR REGULAR ROUTINE, while the missus put on the morning coffee, I headed out back to collect the eggs. I'd done that very thing every day of my life for way more years than I care to contemplate. But today was different. What happened was totally unexpected. And truth be told, a bit unsettling.

No sooner had I opened the back door than this big old blanket of cold mountain mist that had settled in the yard came rolling inside. I can't rightly tell ya why, but I stood there like an addled dunce in the corner of a classroom as it wrapped itself around my ankles and started crawling up my pant legs. Plumb gave me a chill is what it done. Can't say it was a bad chill, just a bit of an unexpected chill. To tell the truth, the only reason I even mention it is because, for a moment there, I was twelve years old again at the old home place. Ma was in the kitchen fixin' breakfast while Pa was out on one of his many long hunts. But that particular long hunt wasn't like any other. It reaped a treasure beyond any we could have imagined.

Well, I guess I probably ought to just go ahead and start at the beginning . . .

ONE

The Homestead

I WAS TO LATER LEARN that Pa first met Diver on the morning of my twelfth birthday. As time would tell, it was a meeting that was to affect myself, my family, and my community in ways we could never have imagined. A true blessing to all. But it very nearly never happened.

The late 1820s and early 1830s saw several families in the Cades Cove region of the Southern Appalachian Mountains merge together to become a true community. Nestled in the western reaches of the Great Smoky Mountains, the valley was officially named Cades Cove, but those of us who lived thereabouts simply called it "the Cove."

On a gently sloping mountainside not far north of

the Cove, comprised of thick woods and rock-strewn meadows, sat the Banion homestead. The cabin was little more than a two-room, hardscrabble log structure with a sleeping loft above and a kitchen and bedroom below. It was divided by a double-faced stone fireplace that served for both heating and cooking. Out back, and well to the left of the stone and grass patch of land we called a yard, sat the necessity. It was a rough-hewn, pine board structure made of loose-fitting slats—"for ventilation," according to Pa. It was hot in summer and cold in winter but boasted a comfortably worn seat that could be brought indoors during inclement weather to save the user from enduring a frost-bitten nether region on a late-night visit.

Far to the right of the yard, near the smokehouse and down a short path bordered by mountain laurels, lay a small family cemetery with a single stone-covered gravesite. It was a lovingly maintained space nestled in a stand of towering pines that always held an aura of hallowed ground to my young mind. Many a day I remember reverently brushing pine needles off the hand-smoothed log bench that faced a small slab of upright sandstone on which was chiseled the simple epitaph, BABY WESTON.

In the front yard of the cabin, out past the rutted trail that led down into the Cove, stood a sturdy, hardwood chicken coop built on thorn-wrapped stilts to help keep critters out.

Perhaps the hardest creatures in the mountains to protect was a good brood of layin' hens... but protect them we did. Ya see, Pa sure did like his fried eggs in the mornin'.

I reckon a bear would have had an easier time gettin' into our cabin than a fox or weasel gettin' into that chicken coop.

Nearby, and within easy distance of the spring-fed creek that ran through our property, was Ma's vegetable garden. It was amazing how much produce she teased out of that little patch of sunny ground. Each fall, our springhouse and root cellar nearly overflowed with fresh, dried, and canned vegetables, not to mention eggs, jams, and wild game.

Ma insisted that Pa's tannin' shed be a fair way down the creek to keep the smell away from the cabin. I reckon anyone who's ever caught a whiff of a freshly brain-tanned hide will understand her concern.

This farm, as humble as it may have been, was the homestead of my father, Zebulon Banion. He'd cut the trees, cleared the land, and built the structures. He'd then crossed the mountains to claim his young bride and brought her home to his wilderness wonderland.

That was many years ago. Since then, Ma, or Kate, as the community called her, gave him four sons and a daughter. Perhaps not the largest family in the region, but respectable none the less. You'd think that should have been about all a young, loving couple could hope for. But the truth is, life was hard and eking out an existence in the mountains even harder.

Pa was a hunter and trapper by trade. To make a living he had to spend long periods of time away from home. And as his family grew, ever more time was required for him to provide. Of course, while providing for is necessary, so is protecting. And as it turned out, protecting was what Ma needed most.

Late one snowy night as Pa stumbled in after a two-week absence, half frozen from a driving north wind and twenty-four hours removed from his last meal, he found the cabin in disarray. Ma had taken ill and lay sprawled across her bed, burning with fever. Young Forrest, the oldest of the Banion boys, had done everything he could think of for both her and baby Weston. But truth be told, he wasn't but a child himself.

"I'm scared, Pa," he said, tears flowing down his cheeks.

Pa rushed to Ma's side and brushed back a strand of lank hair. He then wiped stippled sweat from her brow with a damp rag.

"I tried to get help in the Cove," said Forrest, "but nobody would come. They said they had problems of their own and to try elsewhere."

I think that's the moment Pa changed. The moment he turned his back on his neighbors the same as they'd turned theirs on his family. Some say his heart turned to stone and his soul dimmed. Whatever the case may be, he became a hard, hard man.

It also led to Ma's "low" period. A nearly debilitating case of depression that would follow her, off and on, for the rest of her life.

As time passed, Forrest became a strapping young man. He married Sarah May Wilke and against Pa's wishes, moved out of the hills and into the Cove proper. There, they busied themselves raising three kids of their own.

Pa didn't take kindly to the whole situation, mind you, feeling that Forrest, being the oldest child in the family, should have stuck around and took care of the farm. But as has been the case since the dawn of time, when a young couple feels the urge to spread their wings, they'll leave their mothers and fathers and go out to face the world on their own.

Forrest, having always been a hard worker and possessing a keen mind, soon became foreman of Orwell Beckett's farms, the largest land holdings in the county. He was on his way to becoming one of the most respected and prosperous young men in the Cove.

Casey, Pa's number two son, couldn't have been more different. Two years younger than Forrest, he was wild and independent. He just naturally seemed to gravitate to the wrong elements as soon as he was old enough to sneak out of the house. If trouble was to be had in the region, you could count on Casey and his cohorts being nearby. By sixteen, he was too wild for even Pa to rein in. Then, late one night, without a word of warning, he simply disappeared. Gone without a trace. It would be years before we knew what had happened to him. One more son forsaking the homestead.

Third came Weston, about a year and a half after Casey. He was Ma's little angel. No one can say why a mother takes so strongly to one child above all the rest, but there was no doubt that Weston was the one for Ma. That's what made it all the worse when Ma came down with pneumonia that winter. She got so weak her body could no longer produce the milk needed for the five-month-old baby.

As it happened, a couple from the Ohio Valley by the name of Wheeler had recently moved into the area. They brought along two milk cows and were willing to barter chestnuts and dried blueberries with Pa for fresh sweet milk.

Within twelve hours of receiving the milk poor Weston was dead, as was the cow that gave it.

Years later, Dr. Anna Bixby discovered that the white snakeroot plant, which was widespread throughout the Ohio Valley, was the cause of the dreaded milk sickness. I assume a load of hay brought along on their journey was tainted by the poisonous plant and the cow consumed it. Anyway, Weston's death was what caused Ma's "low" period.

Five years after Weston passed away, Delma came along—beautiful, caring, fun-loving, Delma—the only girl in the Banion Clan. She even melted Pa's heart. The first time I ever saw a tear in the man's eye was the day she married James Chapmere and moved up to Maryville to run the Beckett 'n' Lay General Store.

A full eight years passed after Delma's birth before I came along. Ma wanted to name me Uilleam, after the Earl of Mar, and call me Liam like her great-grandfather. According to family history, Liam was a mighty warrior. Pa shook his head and said, "Billy'll do."

Pa never was keen on our Scottish ancestry for reasons I never did learn, thus our family name: Banion ... without the 'O'.

Coming along nearly a decade after Delma, you might say I was a bit of a surprise. From the way I hear it, Pa was flabbergasted, Ma was plumb worn out, and Delma was overjoyed. She thought I was her very own. And bless her heart if she didn't get me through my younger years as fine as any mother could have. If not for her, I may not have turned out any better than Casey.

Then, when I was eight years old, Delma married James and moved away. I suddenly transitioned from 'little brother' to the reigning child of the Banion homestead. It was an eye-opening experience, and I was more than ready to stake my claim. Now I'm not sayin' I became wild or anything. Ma saw to that. I just became somewhat more independent. Ya see, to my way of thinkin' I was old enough to expand my ventures further into the backwoods, which I did every chance I got. But unfortunately, to Ma's way of thinkin', I was old enough to share in extra chores. I was soon to learn, growing up ain't all fun and games. Now and then life gets in the way.

It was during that time that I first met an Indian boy named Henry Rainwater who was to become my best and truest friend. A kindred soul and fellow explorer. But more on him later.

It was also during that time that I began to take stock in the life my Pa had cut out for us in our cloud-covered hills of the Great Smoky Mountains. Not only the wondrous and happy trails we walked, but the dark and tumultuous paths also.

The summer of my eleventh year was dry. Far too dry. The crops throughout the region suffered greatly as did the animals and home gardens. Unrelenting days of sweat and toil were spent trying to irrigate the field crops and keep the precious homegrown veggies from bolting.

Those with cows and sheep kept them high up on the greener grasses of the bald knobs much later in the fall than usual. It was a risky move, what with the threat of early snow and all, but sometimes there just wasn't nothin' for it. Pigs and goats, on the other hand, were earmarked and released into the hills to fend for themselves. Everyone knew each other's markings and honored the system.

No one foresaw the trouble those actions would lead to, or the changes they would make in so many lives.

On occasion, a sow or goat would come up missing, but bein' open ranged, no one took notice. After all, it's not uncommon for domestic pigs to join

14

up with a passel of wild hogs, and as for goats, well everyone knows they tend to just ramble around unrestricted having no sense of home territory.

It wasn't until two sheep went missing up on Bote Mountain that folks realized there was trouble in the wind. The herder definitely took note, seein's how his pay reflected the welfare of his charges. He soon spread the word and rustled up a search party. When the mangled carcasses were finally found, a thorough investigation of the site took place. Wolves, panthers, and bobcats were all ruled out. With the way the surrounding vegetation was ravaged, there was no doubt a killer bear was in the area.

Word quickly spread and armed men took to the forest. Days passed, then weeks. Livestock continued to disappear, but no sign of the bear was found. Blinds set up near the ambush sites were to no avail as the beast never seemed to return to an old kill.

Most folks figured Pa to be the best tracker in the whole region. Well, perhaps next to an old Cherokee shaman named Two Hand who lived deep in the mountains. But Pa took no interest in the hunt.

"It's not my stock missin'," he said. "Let them rich

folk in the Cove protect their own."

That seemed to be Pa's attitude about anything to do with people from the Cove—or just about anyone else I suppose. He had cleared his own land, built his own cabin and out-buildings, and did for his own family. If others couldn't do the same, they could hightail it back to the city and leave the mountains to mountain folk.

Then, late one night up on Gregory Bald, a young herder named Joey Cobb awakened to the sound of a loud ruckus in the dark. Even through the haze of his dawning consciousness, his befuddled mind grasped the essence of what he was hearing. *A bear was after Mr. Grear's cattle.*

Standing up straight, he cowered near the glow of his dwindling fire. In his hands he grasped the old wired-together flintlock he'd spirited from beneath his father's bed.

Listening as a pitched battle raged, it was almost as if he could picture the confrontation in his mind. One of Mister Grear's cows was putting up a desperate fight. He heard hooves pounding the rock-hard earth as it crashed through the underbrush

16

snapping saplings and uprooting bushes. It bellowed in fear and anger sending great clouds of heated condensation rolling into the night. Horns rattled and clattered in dense thickets as it spun and twisted, blindly thrusting at the dark. Death this night would surely come dearly and through hard-won conquest alone.

Joey listened to the terrible, thunderous roar of the enraged bear as its fury mounted. Shot-like echoes split the darkness as bovine ribs snapped beneath a flurry of pounding blows. Wet sounds washed across the meadow as slabs of bloody meat were slashed from the victim's body. A last mournful bellow engulfed Joey's very being as the confrontation ended with the crash of a heavy body driving into the ground.

A chill rippled across Joey's flesh as the night suddenly fell into a deathly silence. Even the crickets had stilled their persistent hum. It was as if the whole world had stopped to mourn the tragic events that had just played out on that lonesome bald.

Then, out of the darkness came the bear's hoarse, blowing huffs along with the distant receding hoofbeats of frightened cattle dashing to the furthest extremities of the field.

Joey had promised his Ma not to take any chances while on the bald, but he'd also promised Mr. Grear to protect his cattle. The attack weighed heavily on his mind.

I can't just do nothing, he lamented. *If it weren't for Pa being laid up with some kind of blood sickness from a bite received while slaughtering a hog, and if money weren't so tight, Ma never would have agreed to let me come up here in the first place.*

On the other hand, I can't just sit back and let Mister Grear's cows get massacred. After all, few men would've taken a chance on hiring a sixteen-year-old boy to guard their livestock in the first place—no matter how much they needed the money.

"Forgive me, Ma," he whispered. "It's my responsibility."

Joey searched through his woodpile for a pine knot to use as a torch. He then steeled himself against nearly paralyzing fear and quietly stepped out into the dark.

If only the bear had waited a few more days to reach Gregory Bald, Joey's watch would have been over. He wouldn't have been placed in such a dilemma to start

18

with. The skies were gettin' heavy with the threat of snow and the cows would have been herded away.

≈

Thom Grear found what was left of Joey's body two days later as he arrived to drive the cattle off the mountain. Along with the boy, six cow carcasses were scattered across the meadow. The bear must have gone crazy with bloodlust, killing everything that came under its claws. Even after its hunger had long been sated it continued. Killing to kill.

By the time the story made its rounds, even Pa could no longer ignore the threat. This was no ordinary bear. This bear was a killer of men. It was a menace to everyone or everything it came in contact with...including the Banions.

A rage burned in Pa's soul. Man or beast, nothing could be permitted to threaten him or his.

With the deadly determination of a true mountain man, he began to pack for the hunt.

TWO

Gregory Bald

THERE'S NOTHING IN the mountains quite so dangerous as a black bear that has tasted human flesh. They tend to lose all fear of man and simply see him as easy prey. And unlike many other predators, once they start an attack they seldom let up until their victim is dead.

At best, a lone hunter facing such a foe has a single discharge of his flintlock rifle—not the most reliable weapon in tight woodland quarters or hurried conditions, and the thrust of his straight blade knife.

Though it's true that men have walked away from such harrowing encounters, it's rare indeed with a fully mature bear. And even then, they face the lethal probability of infection from filth encrusted claw and fang wounds.

As Pa prepared to pack, a few brave men from the Cove halfheartedly offered to join him in the hunt. He wanted none of it. He was his own man and asked help from no one—at least aside from that night poor Weston died. He did what needed to be done alone, and alone he bore the consequences. Even Forrest's offer was rejected.

Dressed in buckskin trousers, a warm waumases shirt, and a knee-length woolen frock, he strapped his straight-blade knife and hickory-handled hatchet securely around his waist with a heavy piece of rawhide cordage. He then picked up his faithful .40 caliber Pennsylvania long rifle, a powder horn, shot, and patches, before striding into the kitchen.

Ma stood by the table loading corn dodgers and smoked venison into his possibles bag. She then added a tin cup and another strand of braided cord. He nodded his appreciation, then turned so she could help him tie a deerskin ground cover over his broad shoulders.

All these things happened in silence, as they had a thousand times before. Each time Pa ventured out into the wilds could be his last time. But never before had the threat been so real. This time he was going out to face a killer. And only time would tell which of the two would survive.

He then jammed on his old tricorn hat and looked around the room. Glancing at the pine-board counter, he reached out and flipped open an ornately carved wooden box. From inside he removed a twist of tobacco and added it to his bag.

"Might come in handy," he said.

From where I sat on the sagging limb of a yellow buckeye tree, I saw them exit the cabin. Ma stood in the doorway, hands clasped, and head bowed. I suspect she was trying to hide the tears that were freely flowing down her cheeks. Pa, seemingly not knowing what to do, just stood there for a moment. He then leaned down and gave her a kiss on top of the head. Ma threw her arms around him and buried her face in his chest. She then let go and hurried into the cabin. Pa hesitated a moment, then adjusted his hat and strode across the yard.

Our big old Leghorn rooster, a bad-tempered fowl who hated all women except Ma, and chased them

22

every chance he got, scrambled out of Pa's way. His sudden retreat caused a clamor among the hens and for a moment there the yard erupted in a flurry of frightened cackles and flying feathers. But it soon settled back down after the threat had passed.

Striding up to my tree, Pa paused and looked up. For a moment there I thought he was gonna say something. Instead, he simply gave me a nod; a sign of acknowledgment that left me dumbfounded. He then quietly went on his way. That was the first time in my short life I felt a kinship with the man.

Soon the shadows of the forest faded his figure to a silhouette, and he was gone.

≈

Nearly three weeks later, as I lay in my sleeping loft above the kitchen listening to Ma and Pa talk about what had transpired during his absence, he said he'd first headed up onto Gregory Bald to try and pick up the bear's trail. He easily found the site of the slaughter, what with all the dead carcasses, blood, and

23

ripped up underbrush. He said he'd seen less carnage on a battlefield. Of course, the body of young Joey had been removed, but the cattle were left to rot where they fell. It was a total loss for Mr. Grear. "The beasts weren't fit for anything more than feeding the wildlife of the forest and enriching the soil for future growth," was the way he put it.

As Pa examined the ragged wounds on the cows, he was amazed by the width between claw marks. The bear had to be gigantic. Never in all his years had he seen such destruction. Such utter devastation. Even after days of exposure to a myriad of hungry forest critters and carrion eating birds, the carnage was overwhelming.

Most of the cattle had broken necks, shattered ribs, missing legs, and eviscerated stomachs. Pa said he saw entrails ripped from carcasses and flung across the meadow as if seeding a wheatfield. But, oddly enough, two cows had been killed and left totally intact. It was as if by then killing was enough.

He told Ma he'd heard the Cherokee shaman, Two Hand, speak of Silvertip Grizzlies out west that could do such damage, but never a black bear. He'd even found a large patch of blood-soaked soil where the beast had rolled and slithered in the gore as if reveling in the stench of death.

From the looks of the patch, along with the claw marks and bloodied pawprints on the cowhides, Pa figured the bruin must be better than seven-feet-long and possibly weighed eight hundred pounds. Never in his wildest dreams had he ever heard of such a monstrosity roaming the wilds of the Smoky Mountains. And by the looks of it, no man or beast would be safe as long as it did.

Circling the meadow, it hadn't taken Pa long to find the bear's trail into the scrub. Blood-splattered leaves and broken underbrush gave witness to its passing.

Pa was just about to follow when he heard voices in the distance. It sounded like someone coming up the trail from the Cove. He waited a few minutes before seeing flashes of movement through the trees. Four men entering the field. From three-hundred-feet away, he could see it was the Deerborn brothers, Percy Blyth, and a man Pa didn't know.

"What brings y'all up here?" he asked as they

drew near.

"Hey, Zeb," Percy said as he wiped sweat from his brow.

Percy was the only one in the bunch old enough to address Pa by his given name.

"We thought we might find you up here. If you're fixin' to ambush that killer bear when he returns, we thought we'd join ya. Five rifles are better than one."

"Who's this?" Pa asked, nodding at the stranger.

Percy laid his hand on the man's shoulder. "This is Ben Cobb, from over near Tuckaleechee Cove. He's young Joey's cousin. He came to help out, what with Mister Cobb bein' laid up and Joey done taken the way he was. Besides that, ol' Ben here's a mighty fine shot. I don't know if you heard, but old man Grear's placed a forty-dollar bounty on that bear, and Preacher Wilson took up a collection to double it."

"No, I ain't heard," Pa said as he took a quick appraisal of Ben before lookin' back at Percy.

"Well, anyways," Percy continued as he scratched behind his right ear and kinda looked at Pa with unmasked apprehension. "We figured if we took down this brute, we'd give the money to Mister Cobb, him

26

losing his boy and all. Eighty dollars would go a long way toward gettin' 'em through winter."

"Reckon that bear's comin' back, do ya?" Pa asked as he rested his rifle in the crock of his left arm and shifted his tricorn back on his head.

"Well, they usually do, don't they?" asked Percy.

"Yep, I reckon they usually do," said Pa. "But this ain't no usual bear. Way I hear it, it don't come back to its kill sites. Course, this ain't no regular kill site either. There's enough meat scattered around here to draw every critter from a panther to a field mouse. I reckon you boys have about as good a chance here as anywhere."

"Iffen the beast ain't really that ol' shape-shiftin' shaman, like folks been sayin'," said Josh Deerborn in a conspiratorial voice.

"What you talkin' about?" asked Pa. "Who said that about Two Hand?"

"Oh, now, don't get me wrong, Mister Banion," said Josh. "I ain't blamin' the ol' fella . . . I mean, Mister Two Hand. I'm just sayin' that's what some folks down in the Cove's been sayin'."

"Well, I ain't lookin' too kindly on you repeatin'

it," said Pa. "In times like these, it wouldn't take but a small spark fanned by careless tongues to set the whole mountain to blazin'."

"Yeah, I hear ya, Mister Banion," said Josh. "And I'm sure sorry I mentioned it. People sure can get mighty fired up when their afeared and all."

An uncomfortable pause followed as it often did when folks confronted Pa.

Finally, Percy spoke up. "Well, what do you say, Zeb? You gonna throw in with us?"

"No," said Pa. "Reckon not. I'm gonna hit his trail. If he don't turn back and give you boys a shot, I'll just hunker down and dog him to his den, if need be."

Jas Deerborn, who had been standing there fidgeting with his rifle's flint, glanced up at Pa.

"Ah, Mister Banion," he said. "I was just wonderin' . . ." He stopped, looking as if not sure he should finish the thought.

"You was just wonderin' what?" asked Pa.

"Well, sir, about the reward."

"What about it?" Pa's voice was taking on an edge.

"I was just wondering, sir," said Jas, "if he don't come back our way, and you track him down and kill him; well, I was just wonderin' if you might be figurin' to

28

give the reward to the Cobbs? You know, seein's how they're in such need and all."

Pa eyed the young man with an iron glare. "I reckon killin' the beast that killed their boy should lay some comfort on their souls, don't you think? I don't see how robbin' me of mine should play into it. If it were the other way around, you wouldn't see me stealin' the sweat off another man's brow."

Jas and his companions clammed up. They suddenly seemed to find something quite interesting about the tips of their shoes, or maybe that old lightning-struck tree trunk across the way. It's hard sometimes to figure how a man thinks, but when it comes to a man like Pa, it's best to just let it lie.

After a moment, Pa turned and started for the bear's trail. He then stopped and looked back.

"One more thing, boys," he said. "Don't be spreadin' out too far. If that thing does come back this way, he's the biggest beast you ever saw. It's gonna take everything you got to put him down."

The men looked at each other. If Zeb Banion was layin' down a warning, it was wise to stand up and take notice. Somehow the day had just gotten a lot colder. Pa turned and entered the forest alone.

THREE

On The Trail

FOLLOWING THE TRAIL as it departed the glade was no problem. Dried blood still clung to the dark green leaves of thickly clustered laurel trees. Here and there a dogwood sapling, or a small sweetgum tree, was snapped off and pressed to the ground. About a hundred yards farther on, a black walnut tree showed a large muck covered stain where its bark had been rubbed off as the bear vigorously scratched his back against it.

Telltale signs continued through the underbrush. Upturned rocks and flattened vegetation marked the way. Clawed ground and bunched leaves laid testament to ascended slopes and traversed hollows. Pa barely glanced at the evidence to stay on his trail.

Jogging along at a smooth, loping pace, he gained

on the brute. Sprinting down long sloping hillsides, thick with thorny brush and fallen limbs, he barely paused at the bottom before starting up the next incline. He leaped over brooks and splashed through icy streams. Here and there the forest gave way to sweet-smelling mountain glades or blackened lightning burns, before plunging back into the dark recesses of shadow. Long hours were spent attempting to make up ground. His chest heaved and his heart pounded. His rifle and gear strained his arms and back. His legs burned. Still he continued until failing light finally forced his respite.

Having drunk at the last stream he'd crossed, he looked around for a good site to make camp. A half-moon cavity in the ground, hollowed out by the roots of a large fallen tree, seemed to be the perfect spot. It was just about his size and would get him out of the frigid late-fall winds.

After checking to be sure no widowmakers hung from above, he cleared away limbs and rocks that would disturb his rest and drug in great armfuls of leaves to pad his bed. Next, he built a small rock enclosure for a campfire. He then sat back and opened his pack. Supper was smoked venison and corn dodgers.

After satisfying his hunger, he spread his ground cover over the gathered leaves and settled in for a long, cold night.

Dawn broke as a soft glow filtering through a thick mist. Pa sat up and stretched, glancing around in the soupy fog. Visibility was limited to mere feet. Since he knew it was impossible to track in such conditions, he wrapped his frock tighter around his shoulders and chewed on a piece of smoked venison. He waited for the haze to lift.

Last night's fire was reduced to nothing but cold ash with no sparks to rekindle it. Having considered lighting one anew he declined, deciding with the morning dampness it just wasn't worth the effort.

Then, little by little, a light pattering sound of rain began to pelt the forest floor. Soothing and tranquil, it tried to lure him back to sleep—but not for long. Soon, it intensified into a steady drumbeat and rivulets of water began to slowly stream into his sunken berth. If it kept up, it would soon be move or swim. He decided to move.

Gathering his belongings, he found a nearby pine tree with a cluster of overlapping boughs that would give protection from the growing shower. Crawling under, he laid out his ground cover and settled in to wait it out.

The forest by now was a hushed strum of falling rain and pelted leaves. The wall of water around his inadequate redoubt thickened. In the distance, he heard the low rumble of thunder. If he'd been sitting in a raintight shelter, he'd have immensely enjoyed this cleansing of the world. Especially after the long dry summer we had endured. But sitting in the open forest with a persistent drip of cold water running down his back, not so much.

As it so happened, he didn't have to wait long. The rain slowed, dropped to a gentle drizzle, and finally stopped altogether. It was over as quickly as it had begun. Then the mist lifted revealing a fresh pine-scented mountain morning. Pa steeled himself for another long day on the chase.

Day two of the hunt was much the same as day one—only at a much slower pace. Signs of the bear's passing had faded in the last few days, and in places it was completely washed away by the morning's rain.

Pa repeatedly found himself circling back, trying to regain the trail he'd lost. It was an arduous task, calling upon all the wilderness skills he had acquired in a lifetime of roaming the mountains. Very few woodsmen could have accomplished what he had already. By the day's end, he was following more by hunches and instinct than by any actual signs.

A few dried berries found along the way, two corn dodgers, a slice of smoked venison jerky, and a long cold drink from a nearby stream made do for supper. He readied for bed.

Day three on the trail started slow and ended as a total bust. At one point he saw black fur moving through the timber, but after he circled 'round to lay in wait, an adolescent bear came shambling into view. Being much too small to be the bruin he was after, he let it meander away, not knowing how close to death it had come.

34

By nightfall Pa was tired, frustrated, and out of corn dodgers. He curled up near a small fire and spent a cold night under the low-hanging branches of an eastern mountain hemlock.

Morning arrived with another crisp, cold mist. Not at all unusual for the high mountain elevations. This one floated a good eight feet off the ground.

Pa, sore from a pestersome twig that had gouged his ribs all night, slowly crawled from under his hemlock abode and stretched. He noted the mist was high enough to allow the search to continue. If there had been a clue of which way to continue.

There wasn't.

Reaching into his possibles bag, he removed the last of his aging, strong-smelling venison, and began to gnaw on it. His mind fantasized about the soft crunch of his long-gone corn dodgers. He would need to replenish his rations soon, but first he needed to formulate a strategy to continue the hunt. He'd lost the trail, and rambling around the mountains wasn't going to solve his dilemma.

After some thought, he settled on a plan. He wasn't far from Bear Shoal Hollow, the home of Two

Hand, the Cherokee shaman. If anyone knew how to find this bear it would be Two Hand.

You couldn't pay most folks from the Cove to rendezvous with the old shaman. Some said he was a shapeshifter. Some thought he was ageless. Pa grinned at the thought. He'd known Two Hand since; well, since before he'd even come to the Cove. Since before most anybody had come to the Cove, for that matter.

Pa and Two Hand had hunted, fished, and trapped together. Watched each other's backs. He remembered the winter Chief Doublehead sent his Creek assassins into the mountains to capture or kill Two Hand. Eight Creek warriors entered the Smokies. Only three wounded, frightened men returned home. Pa and Two Hand had survived without a scratch and the shapeshifter legend grew.

Pa knew Two Hand to be a fine, upstanding man and a true friend. Perhaps the only friend he'd had other than an old trapper that Ma despised. But a shapeshifter? Pa could only shake his head. As for Two Hand, he just chuckled about the notion and did nothing to discourage the myth.

Now when it came to being timeless, even Pa was not real sure. His first memory of Two Hand was from when he first journeyed to the Smokies as a young hunter. He came following a tale he'd been told as a child; a story of his own rescue by a giant Indian on the day the rest of his family died. A giant who was said to be living in the Great Smoky Mountains.

As is the way with youth, he had foolishly gotten himself into a predicament that could have led to his demise. Then, out of nowhere, Two Hand appeared. He stood there looking down at Pa, prostrate beneath a huge slab of shifted granite pinning him to the ground. It appeared he was trying to decide if helping was worth his effort.

To Pa, Two Hand looked well-advanced in age. He bore the semblance of a mythical giant from some ancient Greek legend.

"You comfortable under there?" asked the giant.

"No," said Pa. "I'd truly appreciate some help, if it's ain't too much to ask."

"Why are you here?" asked the Indian.

"I was just huntin'," said Pa. Which was true. He didn't mention he was hunting both game and a legend. "Tried to climb the outcrop here, and when it broke loose, I found myself as you see me."

"Ever heard of a Cherokee Chief by the name of Doublehead?" the Indian asked.

"Yeah, I've heard of him," answered Pa, "but I've never met the man."

"So, he did not send you here?" The giant asked with flinty eyes.

"I wouldn't know him if I saw him," said Pa. "Like I said, I was just huntin'."

With that, Two Hand wrapped his enormous fingers around a protrusion in the stone and using strength Pa could only marvel at, lifted the large slab of granite off of him. He then tipped it over and let it go. It slammed to the ground with a thundering crash and a puff of dust.

"They call me Two Hand," the Indian said as he reached out and helped Pa to his feet.

Pa patted himself down to make sure nothing was broken as he said, "I'm Zebulon Banion, and I thank you, Two Hand. You saved my life."

From that day forward, Pa and Two Hand had been faithful companions.

≈

Taking his bearings, Pa headed for Bear Shoal Hollow and a reunion with the shaman. It would be good to see his old friend.

Upon arriving, he laid his ground cover and hunting gear under a rocky overhang at the entrance of the canyon. Even though he and the shaman were like father and son, he didn't presume to enter Two Hand's domain uninvited.

Gathering enough dry wood to cook his supper and maintain an overnight fire, he strolled down to the swift flowing stream to fish. Using his hatchet, skinning knife, and a leather fringe, he fashioned a three-pointed fishing spear. He then cut a long, thin, slice of rancid venison, pierced it with a foot long stick, and anchored it in the eddy before him. The goal was to make a smelly lure that looked and sounded like a small creature bobbing and swirling in the current as if in distress. Brook trout aren't finicky eaters and will snatch up nearly anything edible they come across. Pa then positioned himself in the shadows of a rhododendron bush near the stream's edge and waited.

Before long, a nice trout worked its way up the stream investigating any flotsam that happened to wash by.

Pa cocked his arm back.

The fish, as if sensing something wasn't right, hesitated. It then sank down next to a moss-covered boulder. In the shaded current it was nearly invisible.

Pa stood stone still.

After a long pause, the fish slowly drifted forward.

One quick thrust and a flip of his wrists sent the beginning of Pa's supper well back onto the stream bank. He grinned and prepared for the next challenge. Twenty minutes and two more thrusts saw him with his evening meal.

After enjoying a well-deserved feast of blackened brook trout and wild onions, Pa pitched the remains into the stream so as not to draw predators. He then washed up, banked his fire, and settled in for a cozy night. He had positioned the fire in such a way as to have the heat radiate off the overhang and create a comfortable shelter. Being drained after a long day, he was soon fast asleep.

In the wee hours of morning, so stealthily that not even Pa detected him, a visitor entered camp. When Pa awoke to the last twinkling stars, the first thing he noticed was the ancient, gap-toothed grin of old Two Hand sitting across the fire from him.

"Zebulon," the giant said. "When you did not rise with the noon sun, I feared you had gone to be with the Creator. I nearly covered you with stones to honor your remains and took the walk of sorrow to your woman."

"Very funny, Grandfather," Pa said. "The only reason you're up and about to hassle me this early in the mornin' is 'cause you ancient ones just don't need sleep."

Two Hand laughed. "It's good to see you, Zeb," he said.

"And you," said Pa. "It's been too long."

Pa then threw back his ground cover and excused himself as he ambled off into the woods. When he returned, Two Hand had a more serious look on his face.

"I suppose you're here about the bear," he said.

"Yes sir," said Pa. "It's done killed young Joey Cobb, and I reckon if it's not stopped it'll kill again."

"You know," said Two Hand, "some folks claim it was me in bear form what killed that boy."

Pa was a bit taken aback.

"Yeah, I've heard the talk," he said. "But I'll be if I know how you heard it way out here."

The shaman shrugged.

"But it serves ya right," continued Pa. "Egging on that shapeshiftin' business and all. You know, one of these days that old myth is gonna get you hung."

"That may be," said Two Hand, "but so far it's come in handy."

"Anyway," said Pa, "I need to pick up the trail of that killer bear, and I was hoping you could help me out."

Two Hand thought about it for a minute. He then flicked a tick off his sleeve.

"I reckon if it were me lookin' for that bear," he said, "I'd head on over to Pointin' Rock. It seems to spend a lot of time in that region so it just may have a den up near there."

Pointin' Rock was a stone outcropping at the head of a thickly wooded high mountain valley. It had a long, slender piece of gneiss rock protruding from its face that resembled a finger pointin' down the valley.

Pa and Two Hand had spent more than one star-filled night camped out under that huge finger while listening to the coyotes sing their age-old song to the moon.

"I appreciate that," said Pa as he reached into his possibles bag. He withdrew the twist of tobacco and handed it to the old shaman. "I figured you might be gettin' a bit low."

Two Hand gratefully accepted the gift.

"It's in times like these that I'm glad I didn't leave you under that slab," he said with a grin.

He then reached out and laid his massive hand on Pa's shoulder.

"May the Creator watch over you and guide you on your quest," he said. Then he turned and walked away.

After Two Hand's departure, Pa gathered-up his belongings and made his way out of the hollow. As he rounded the shoulder of a rocky column, he noticed a deerskin pouch hanging from the branch of a tree. Retrieving it, he loosened the rawhide cord that held it shut. Inside was a large slice of freshly smoked venison, several strips of pemmican, and four pieces of frybread.

Pa smiled and slung the strap of the pouch over his left shoulder.

He silently thanked his friend.

FOUR

Laurel Hell

EARLY EVENING FOUND PA sitting on his ground cover nestled in below Pointing Rock. He had a sheltered fire crackling nearby; built with dry kindling he and Two Hand had stashed under the prominence during a long-ago visit. Light wisps of smoke gently swirled around the grotto before slowly ascending up and around the finger to dissipate in the fresh breeze above.

Pa reached up and traced his finger along the crudely carved initials he and Two Hand had discovered in the grotto wall many years before: 'MZ'. He once again wondered if they might truly belong to the legendary outcast, Moss Zeekman?

Moss had been an indentured servant in Boston who'd been denied his "freedom dues" when his years of servitude had been completed. It was claimed in court that he'd damaged "precious cargo" by mishap and owed an additional ten years in recompense. Being a man of no means, while his wealthy master was well-placed, he was convicted and sentenced to the additional term.

Waiting eleven months for an opportunity, he finally made his escape while hauling freight in the lower Appalachians. It was said he survived twelve years alone in the mountains before discovering a vein of gold worth more than his previous master's entire fortune . . . many times over.

He then made a trip back to Boston where he exchanged several gold nuggets for Spanish escudos and purposefully dispersed the coins throughout the city to flaunt his wealth. Having thus attained the attention he so desired, he then hired the most prestigious law firm in the region to both clear his own name, and forever blacken the reputation of the merchant who had oppressed him so egregiously. Upon accomplishing his goal, he disappeared back into the mountains, never to be seen by white men again.

Some say he was adopted into an Indian tribe. Some say he was murdered by thieves. All anyone really knows is that neither he nor his gold ever returned from his wilderness retreat. And though his gold mine has never been rediscovered, many a man has squandered his life in fruitless searches through the mountains of Georgia, North Carolina, and Tennessee in search of it.

As Pa sat back enjoying a supper of venison, frybread, and spruce tea, he listened to the conversations of nature. Squirrels chattering in the hardwoods, an ovenbird trilling his song in the far-off distance, a forlorn male elk bugling his declaration of dominance over his domain. All seemed right with the world.

Before long, with the music of the mountains in his ears, and the soft glow of the November sun quickly fading behind a towering peak, he stretched out on his back with his hands folded over his stuffed belly and peacefully dozed off into a dreamless sleep.

Abruptly he awoke. A feeling of unease engulfed him. He had no idea what had awakened him, but the forest was oddly hushed. The crisp night air was uncommonly silent as if the forest was holding its breath in anticipation. Then in the distance he heard a roar. It was followed by another, somewhat softer reply. Then the first again. After that, it became a snarling, growling, free-for-all cacophony of sound. Pa knew he was listening to the clash of two enraged bears as they battled for dominance.

Sound carries a great distance in cool night air, so Pa placed the fight somewhere at the far-end of the valley. He listened for several minutes before the noise suddenly stopped. Quiet returned to the mountains. He sat there for quite some time. Then, in the flickering light of his half-banked fire, he saw the gentle flutter of lightly falling snow. Tossing a few more sticks on the fire, he wrapped his frock tightly around his shoulders and nestled in as he watched the delicate flakes descending to the ground below. Only in the mountains it seemed, could the fury of a deadly battle be so interlaced with the beauty of nature. Being a man comfortable in his element, he dozed off again.

Waking to a clear cold morning, Pa sat up and stirred the ashes in his stone ring. Finding a few small embers that had lasted the night, he placed a handful of birch twigs over them and gently blew a small flame to life. He then gradually added fuel to the fire until he sat before a warming blaze.

All about his sheltered retreat the world glistened with a light blanket of freshly fallen snow from the night's flurry. A sudden chill convinced him that when nature calls man must answer. Rising and stretching his stiff, chilled muscles, he shuffled from his shelter and used a nearby bush as a necessity. He then trotted down to the spring to wash his face and hands in the icy water before returning to the fire, somewhat numb, but vastly relieved.

He munched on a cold breakfast of frybread and pemmican. Then, not willing to risk facing the bear with questionable powder, he cleared the barrel of his rifle and rammed a fresh load home. Finally, after dousing the fire, he followed a game trail into the valley.

≈

Late morning found Pa crouched behind a thick wall of cattails at the edge of an acre or so of swampy woodland. The area couldn't have been more devastated if a tornado had touched down. Small trees were snapped in half, fallen limbs were crushed and twisted, and patches of grass and soil were ripped from the ground.

Beyond the clearing lay a large stretch of laurel hell—dark and foreboding in its twisted mess of clinging limbs and vines. But what held Pa's attention was a large mass of mangled flesh and bloodied hair lying twisted in the tangled limbs of a blown-down tree. Even at a distance, Pa could see it was a massive adult black bear. Splotchy gray hair on its face and muzzle spoke of age, but muscle mass indicated enormous power. That another creature could have destroyed such a monarch of the woods was nearly unimaginable.

Carefully scanning every inch of the surrounding forest, Pa searched for any evidence that the killer was still nearby. He didn't look for a body. Seldom is a whole body visible in the backwoods. He looked for the oval shape of an ear, or the wet glint of an eye.

50

Perhaps a spot in the shadows that was darker than its surroundings. No unaccountable objects could be seen.

Even feeling confident in his observation, Pa still didn't move. He closed his eyes and listened for any unnatural sounds: a breath, a huff, the soft snap of a twig underfoot. He even tried to discern the difference between windblown leaves and those rustled by an advancing foe.

Once again, the area seemed deserted.

Finally satisfied with both sight and sound, he slowly inhaled a deep telling breath through his nose. It was an old Indian trick he'd learned from Two Hand. Most white men don't realize how often an Indian will detect game or an enemy from scent alone.

Satisfied no danger lurked in the immediate vicinity, he slowly rose and reexamined the area one more time. From his vantage point he saw the ripped and gouged battleground, the downed tree harboring the mangled remains, and all the other remnants of the struggle. Then his attention resettled on the laurel hell.

A *hell* is a large, tangled mass of rhododendrons

51

so thick a man can barely cut his way through it. In some locations they can cover many acres of ground, and it's not uncommon for a man to slash his way through for an entire day and not travel a quarter mile. Yet, what Pa observed was a dark tunnel smashed and ripped through this hell as if the bear had considered it a mere inconvenience. Too much bother to go around. The sheer brute-force it took to accomplish such a deed was awe inspiring.

With the greatest of care, and no little trepidation, Pa eased his way across the clearing and into the tunnel-like trail. Holding the stock of the flintlock well back under his arm to shorten the length of the barrel, he tried to keep it from getting tangled in the brush. This made it impossible to aim, but in these tight quarters any attack would come so fast, at best he would only have time to point and shoot anyway.

On he went for what seemed like hours. Every foot fall was placed toe first, easing it down to give him the ability to make any adjustments necessary to prevent the least sound in the scattered ground litter. Every limb was avoided, so as not to scrape along his clothing or gear. Care even had to be taken when occasionally moving a waxy laurel leaf from his path, to prevent a flash or glimmer of sunlight which might reveal his presence.

As he neared the far edge of the laurel hell, he began to hear the faint sound of falling water. With each step the sound grew louder. He knew that it helped mute his approach, but it silenced any sound the bear might make also. Advantages had been lost to both predator and prey. And truth be told, in this struggle, Pa wasn't sure which was which. Though he was not often a praying man, he had a prayer on his lips as he continued.

Then, almost without warning, he was out of the tunnel and into the open forest.

Free of the close confines, he inhaled the cool mountain air. It seemed like hours since he'd had a full breath. Or seen beyond arm's length either.

As he took in the sites, the only sound he heard was the distant roar of falling water far ahead.

Calling upon all the stealth he possessed, he continued through the open landscape, straining his eyes in all directions. Nothing seemed out of the ordinary, yet a cold shiver coursed down his back. He didn't know how he knew the bear was nearby, but he had no doubt that it was. A man did not survive long in the wilderness without heeding his inner warnings.

Another hundred yards brought Pa to the rocky bank of a swiftly flowing stream. Being parched from long hours of tense exertion, he thoroughly scanned his surroundings one more time before placing his possibles bag and rifle on the ground so he could crouch down and get a drink of ice-cold water. Having thus quenched his thirst, he stretched out his arm to retrieve his gear...and froze. There, between two moss covered rocks, was the same enormous paw print he'd seen in the clearing on Gregory Bald. The track was indisputable.

Still astonished at the size of the imprint, he watched as a small pebble pressed up between two claw marks slowly gave way and slid to the bottom of the muddy impression. His trepidation was justified. The bear had stopped to drink at the water's edge no more than an hour before. It was close.

Carefully, Pa followed the riverbank up stream. His keen eyes noted every freshly tilted rock, or smudged clump of moss. He saw every water-filled

54

depression in the loose gravel, and every muddy strand of obsidian black hair clinging to fallen logs that the beast had dragged its enormous bulk across.

On went the search, and louder grew the torrent of falling water.

Finally, as the sun was beginning to sink low in the sky, Pa came to a clearing below an eighty-foot waterfall. He recognized the feature from a previous hunt. The brush choked trail angled up the right side of the embankment before circling back at the top of the ridge and ending near the lip of the cascade.

As he watched, he noticed small trees and bushes shaking as if a large body was ascending the slope.

Confident he had finally found his prey, he freshened the powder in his flash pan, propped his tricorn hat in the crotch of a tree, and steadied his weapon on a low-hanging limb while waiting for the beast to show itself. His Pennsylvania rifle had an effective range of well over three hundred yards. Even at an uphill angle he couldn't miss. The shot was as good as made.

Time slowed. On the slope all movement stopped. Pa waited. With the concentration of a born hunter, his attention never wavered. He'd know when to pull the trigger. From where the trail turned back on itself, he saw a glimmer of silky black hair. It was too deep in the brush to get a clear shot. He waited. His time would come. Again and again, he spotted the bear, but always it was obscured just enough to deny a sure shot. *Wait for the last twenty yards*, he thought. There was an unobstructed spot. That would be the kill zone.

From the corner of his eye, Pa noticed another movement. Something coming through the trees above the falls. It was on a direct collision course with the bear. As Pa watched, a man leading a mule came through a barren space in the woods. The bear raised its head and sniffed. Pa didn't have a clear shot. Within seconds they'd come face to face.

Pa stood and waved his rifle, shouting as loud as he could. It was a futile gesture. There was no way to make himself be heard over the roar of the plunging cascade. Readjusting his aim, Pa waited for the bear to step into the clearing. As fate would have it, the man entered first.

The instant the man and mule came into view, the

bear charged. Panicked, the mule spun trying to get away. Purely by chance, he placed himself between the man and the beast. It happened in an instant, though to Pa it seemed like slow motion. He saw every movement. The mule reared; the bear slashed out nearly taking the creature's head off. Pa fired.

A puff of dust exploded from the brute's side even as the mule crashed to the ground and the man was flung into the torrent of water.

Pa missed most of the action after his shot because of the flash in his pan and the billowing smoke from the rifle's barrel, but when the smoke cleared the bear was gone, the mule was obscured by the lip of the ridge, and the stranger was plunging head over heels down the falls. He was smashed and dragged over protruding rocks as he went. From Pa's vantage point, it appeared to be a brutal descent, probably fatal. Halfway down the man cleared the last obstacle and was in free fall to the icy pool below. His body plunged into the frothy wash and was driven beneath the surface. Seconds passed. The stranger didn't emerge.

Pa knew objects often got caught up in the jagged

rocks and churning water below falls and stayed for hours, even days.

If this man was to have any chance at all, he would have to go in and pull him out. Hopefully, not drowned.

But to do so could mean losing the bear.

To most men the choice would be obvious. But Pa wasn't most men. It took him a second or two to decide.

FIVE

Come See What I Brung Ya

PA PROPPED HIS LONGRIFLE against a tree and threw off his gear. Then running to the pool, he paused to discard his frock coat and shirt before plunging into the frigid water. Slammed by the cold, with his heart pounding in his chest, he fought the turbulent current, desperately searching for the stranger.

It was impossible to keep oriented, even as to what was up and what was down. The swirling surge was irrepressible, and before long Pa realized the best thing he could do was attempt to save himself. But suddenly his hand grasped a wad of sodden material, and a quick tug of his arm assured him he had found the man.

Frantically glancing around, he saw a glimmer of

sunlight through the churn. Then pushing off from the rocky bed of the pool, he thrust himself and his charge toward the surface. With a huge gasp of air, he refilled his lungs as he burst forth from the deep. Then, crawling along on nearly frozen hands and knees, he quickly dragged the stranger onto dry ground.

Pa draped the man face down over a dead tree and beat on his back until he spewed out an impressive amount of liquid. He then gasped in life-giving air.

Though breathing, the stranger was unconscious and violently shivering in the cold fall air. Pa quickly stripped him of his wet clothing and patted him dry with his own warm waumases shirt. He then wrapped him in his frock coat and deerskin ground cover. That done, Pa gathered an armful of kindling to arrange near the prostrate stranger. He then rushed to his discarded gear and snatched up his powder horn and rifle. Upon returning to the pile of wood, he doused it with black powder, triggered the rifle's flint, and sparked the fire into life.

By this time Pa was nearly frozen himself, so he

quickly put on his damp shirt, then removed his wet trousers and moccasins. Wringing out all the wet clothing, he arranged them around the fire to dry. Checking one more time to see that the stranger was still breathing, he stood like a vertical rotisserie by the fire, rotating front to back to front, basking in the heat.

After what felt like hours, he redressed in slightly damp, though luxuriously warm pants and moccasins. He knew they would finish drying from his body heat alone. He then searched along the base of the cliff for shelter.

He soon found an overhang that would suffice. It was only about three feet tall, but it was plenty deep to get them out of any possible weather. It wasn't long before he had shifted the stranger and their goods to the new shelter with a cozy fire going.

Finally having time for a more thorough examination of the man, Pa set to work. He found the stranger had a badly swollen left knee, a dislocated right hip, and scrapes and bruises over much of his body. There was a large contusion just behind his right ear, and his left arm was broken slightly below the elbow.

Splitting a straight piece of dried wood with his hatchet and using deerskin cordage from his possibles bag, he set the arm and fashioned a splint. Then, carefully wedging his foot into the man's crotch, he grabbed his right ankle and gave a mighty yank to snap his hip back into place. In his comatose state, the stranger groaned but didn't open his eyes. Pa figured that was for the best as it saved him a heap of pain.

After eating a quick supper and dribbling a little water down the man's throat, Pa stretched out on the shelter's flat-rock floor and slipped into an exhausted sleep. By then it was dark, and there was nothing more to be done.

Morning brought a clear but very cold dawn. After checking on his patient, Pa built up the fire and ate a slice of venison with a little pemmican for breakfast. The frybread unfortunately was gone. Then taking his rifle and fixin's, he headed up the ridge trail hoping to find a very dead, very large bear.

Upon cautiously reaching the site of the previous night's conflict, Pa was bitterly disappointed. While the mule lay partially in the water and partially on the bloody shore, the bear was nowhere in sight.

Following the edge of the stream back the way the man had come, Pa found where the brute had left the trail and barreled headlong through the underbrush, ripping and tearing as if in a rage. Pa followed the well-defined path of destruction for several hundred yards until it became quite obvious that the beast was not stopping or even slowing down. Either the .40 caliber ball had not penetrated deep enough to be fatal, or the bear would go off to some distant haunt and die alone. If not for the injured man, Pa would have trailed it to ground; but what could he do, let the man die?

Fool cost me eighty bucks, he thought to himself.

Returning to the mule, Pa checked to see what was salvageable. Unfortunately, the sawbuck and panniers were lost in the attack. They were most likely washed over the falls and ended at the bottom of the pool. Pa didn't relish the thought of going back in there, so what was lost was lost.

He retrieved a saddle blanket that had somehow wound up snagged in a thorny bush, and he cut loose the lead rope and harness from the mule. With a quick scan of the nearby area, he saw a shovel with a broken handle and nothing else of value. At first he didn't think what he recovered was worth the effort it took to make the climb up the rise, but as it turned out the items he found proved useful.

Taking the rope, harness, and blanket, he returned to camp. The stranger was still lying where Pa had left him, but now his eyes were open.

"Morning," said Pa.

The man just stared.

"I'm Zeb Banion," he tried again. "I just so happened to witness your run-in with that bear."

Still no reply.

"What's your name?" Pa asked.

The man had a bewildered expression on his face as he shook his head and said, "I don't know."

"You don't know?" said Pa. "I reckon that tumble over the falls done rattled ya a bit. I wouldn't worry none though. It'll come back to ya." Pa speared a couple pieces of half frozen venison and propped them over the fire. "In the meantime, I'll call ya . . . I don't know. . . yes, I do. After seein' ya come flyin' down that fall the way ya did, I'll call ya Diver. What do ya think?"

The stranger just sat there.

"Well then, Diver it is," said Pa.

With great difficulty they finally got Diver dressed, though they had to cut one sleeve off his shirt and put a long slit in his left pant leg to do so. Luckily, he had been wearing a poncho, so it could be worn without alterations.

Though obviously in a great deal of pain throughout that day, the man never complained. Pa saw to it that he had plenty to eat and drink, but conversation was scarce. Not only had he forgotten his name, but also where he was from, and why he was there.

"You just rest up for now, Diver," Pa said. "Tomorrow we'll figure a way to get out of here."

Pa knew they were in real trouble. It could be weeks before Diver was able to walk, and that flurry the other night was just a prelude to what could be

65

coming. While not knowing the true extent of the man's injuries, getting trapped by a Smoky Mountain snowstorm could spell disaster. But, what to do?

By late evening Pa had come up with a plan. Not a good plan, but the only one he could come up with.

"A couple miles south of here, I know where a dead bear is," he told Diver. "Come mornin', I'm gonna go skin him. If he ain't turned too bad, I might even get a back strap off him. Then I'll build a travois using your saddle blanket, and you'll have that bear hide to keep you from freezing to death. Then I reckon we'll be gettin' outta here."

"It ain't possible," said Diver. "No one could pull a man through these mountains on a travois."

"It ain't for you to be saying," said Pa. "I figure it ain't more than thirty or so miles to my cabin, and I'm fixin' to try for it."

The next day was spent preparing for the trip.

Pa retrieved the bearskin and a nice slab of meat, kept fresh by the cold weather. He built a drying rack over a glowing pile of embers, and Diver went to work slicing the slab into thin strips.

While Diver did what he could, Pa constructed the

hand-pulled travois out of two strong saplings and the saddle blanket. He used deer hide cordage and harness straps to tie it together. The lead rope would make a good shoulder strap, and he wrapped the handle ends of the saplings in bear skins to help keep from chafing his hands.

That night Diver would sleep in the strong-smelling bear hide and the next day it would be tied on the travois to keep him warm on the journey. Pa would have no trouble staying warm once the work began.

With the travois completed, Pa hung strips of bear meat over the smoldering embers to dehydrate.

≈

Four days of hard work finally brought them to Anthony's Creek Trail. As they made camp, built a fire, and prepared a meal of strong bear jerky and pemmican scraps, Pa told Diver they'd be home the next day. In all that time, Diver's memory had not returned. He had no problem with rational thought;

in fact, he seemed to be a learned man. But when it came to home, family, or personal history, he was at a total loss. Yet even with his faulty recall, his injured body, and the agonizing pain of being bounced along on a travois in that inhospitable mountain wilderness, he never complained. Pa was impressed and found he enjoyed the man's company. Something he had never experienced with another soul, save Kathryn and Two Hand, in the past thirty-some years.

The journey, though quite arduous for both Pa and Diver, was relatively smooth. Pa did lots of exploring to find travois accessible routes, and he made wide sweeping detours to avoid the steeper hillsides. The toughest, and most dangerous obstacles they faced, were the fast-flowing streams.

Deep stretches of water were uncrossable. They had to be avoided. Some swift sections were manageable, but only if a good ford was found. When in question, Pa would first remove his trousers to keep them dry and traverse the stream with only the gear on his back to test the crossing. If it was suitable, he would leave his gear on the bank and re-cross to bring Diver over on his strong broad back. He'd then

68

make a third trip for the bear skin, and a fourth for the travois itself.

Four round trips with Pa bare legged in nearly freezing water. It was a task few men could have accomplished and even fewer would have tried. On the third day of the journey two such crossings were required.

Yet the saving grace in the whole ordeal was the weather. No rain, no snow, no ice. A snowstorm of any real size might have doomed the whole trek. Had the ground been slick and the travois weighed down with built-up snow under it, even Pa may have found the task impossible. But for Pa to have carried Diver, it would have meant leaving the bear skin and all Pa's gear. Pa may have survived the cold mountain nights, but Diver, in his weakened state? Well, it was doubtful.

As night approached and Pa cut saplings and pine boughs to build a lean-to, he and Diver reminisced about the ordeal they had just come through and what the morrow would bring.

Pa said, "It's mostly downhill from here, and there are no more streams that a man couldn't jump across."

Diver responded, "I don't figure I'll be stream jumping for quite some time."

Pa chuckled.

"Well, at least it ain't snowed," Pa said.

No sooner had the statement left his mouth than a large white flake fluttered down and settled on Diver's bear skin covered leg.

Startled, the two men looked at each other and then burst out laughing.

"Don't make no more observations," said Diver. "You'll sink us yet."

Pa laughed so hard his eyes began to water in the crisp, cold air. Then as more snow gently fell, he hurried to finish the shelter.

Later, warmed by a crackling birchwood fire, they sat watching as a white blanket of snow quietly spread out across the forest floor.

"Don't matter now," Pa said. "Can't be but six miles to the homestead, and most of it's downhill. If I can't pull ya, I'll carry ya."

"Well, let's hope that pulling will do," said Diver. "Don't want to offend you none, but I'd rather ride a spiky-haired wild boar than be carried on no man's back for six miles."

Pa smiled. "And if I had me a spiky-haired wild boar, I'd sure let you do it."

With that both men chuckled, laid down, and drifted off to sleep.

To Pa's relief, morning revealed a light dusting of snow on the ridge lines with perhaps a few inches in the valleys. Certainly not enough to wrestle down no spiky-haired wild boar for Diver to ride.

Breakfast was cold and quick. When Pa took what little meat remained from his possibles bag, the odor alone was enough to convince him it was well past its prime. The naturally dark strips of black bear backstrap had become a bit slimy to the touch, and it exuded a far too gamey smell for Pa's liking. With some animals you could push your luck a bit, but not with bears. They had a nasty habit of bitin' ya back when kept too long or not prepared right. Best to just go ahead and throw it out, which is what Pa did.

That left the last of the venison that Two Hand had given him so generously. Having been slow smoked over a hickory fire it was still appetizing even after more than a week on the trail. In fact, it was quite savory.

After breakfast, they hit the trail. It was an easier track, and they made good time. They were following a well-used path the Cove herders had established years before to drive their cattle to and from the high mountain meadows each spring and fall. And like Pa said, since they were coming off the mountains, it was mostly downhill.

Around lunchtime they took their only break. It was at a scenic little waterfall and gave Pa a much-needed breather from the pulling. Diver was just as ready for a respite from the bouncing.

Later that evening they entered Pa's holdings. There was one final creek to cross, but Pa just went ahead and pulled straight through. He then skirted around a small grove of hemlocks and their journey was over.

"Kathryn!" Pa called out as the cabin came into view. "Kathryn! Come see what I brung ya."

SIX

Diver

I HAD A BUNCH OF SNARES placed around the homestead that had caught me two rabbits that mornin'. Ma acted like she was plenty tickled with 'em and allowed how she'd developed a mighty hankerin' for rabbit stew just lately. I told her how I thought that sounded like a fine idea to me. Not bein' much of a bookhound herself, she then asked me to read her somethin' while she worked.

"Sure," I said.

One of the many things Delma instilled in me before she got married was a love of reading. For that, I'll be eternally grateful.

So, while Ma cut vegetables, divided rabbit, and boiled water, I laid on a reed mat next to the fireplace and read *The Legend of Sleepy Hollow* to her.

I'd read the book once before in school, but I liked it so much I asked my teacher, Miss Melloncamp, if I could take it home to read again. She was mighty careful 'bout her books cause they were hard to come by, but I guess she was so pleased that I had finally taken an interest in something that she agreed to let me borrow it.

Anyway, I was at the part where Ichabod Crane had just left the van Tassel farm and was all wound up and nervous and such, when I heard a callin' coming from outside. At first, I wasn't sure if I'd really heard somethin', or if I was just anticipatin' the headless horseman gettin' after ol' Ichabod.

Ma, on the other hand, knew exactly what she'd heard. She'd waited for that sound for the last three weeks. With a little gasp in her throat, she tossed her paring knife into the bowl on the table, jumped up and dashed for the door.

In an instant, I was right behind her. Out the door we went, and around the corner of the cabin we ran. We stopped for just a moment before seein' Pa over near the springhouse. It looked like he was pulling a big ol' bear on a couple of limbs.

"You got 'em, Pa?" I shouted as I crossed the yard.

"Well, I got somethin'," Pa said. "But it ain't what you think."

I ran up and nearly tripped over my own feet when I saw what Pa was pulling. It wasn't no bear at all. It was a man! A man wrapped in a bear skin! He was holdin' Pa's rifle and smilin' up at me.

"You must be Billy," the man said. "Glad to meet ya. Your pa's told me quite a bit about you and your ma."

I'm not sure what startled me more, the fact that Pa was pulling a bear skin wrapped stranger across the yard, or that Pa would have mentioned my name to him. I just kinda stood there, starin', and noddin' my head. Hey, I had just turned twelve years old, and I didn't know a thing about strangers.

Anyway, by this time Pa had set down his load. He gave Ma a hug and a kiss on top of her head when she rushed into his arms. I could tell he was a bit uncomfortable, not being one to show emotion in front of others and all.

"Zeb, you're back," Ma cried. "You had me so worried. You've been gone for so long, I thought . . .

well, I don't even want to say what I thought. But you're back now."

She gave him another hug.

He gently extracted himself from her embrace and motioned toward the stranger on the ground. I don't think she'd even noticed him.

"Kathryn, I'd like you to meet Diver," he said.

"Diver?" Ma was bewildered by such a name.

Pa grinned. "I'll explain it all later. It's quite a story. But for now, we need to get Diver inside by a warm fire. He's hurt bad, and the last few days ain't been easy on him."

Ma looked down at the man and could see the pain etched in his face. It was something that couldn't be hidden by the pleasant smile, though try he did.

"Evening, Ma'am," he said. "I sure do hate to be puttin' you out any."

"Oh, hooey," Ma said.

I believe hooey was the strongest language I ever heard in our cabin.

Turning to Pa she said, "Zeb, get him outta these trappin's, and lay him on the mat by the fire."

She then glanced at me. "Billy, grab a bucket and

get me some spring water."

With that she grabbed up her long skirt and rushed back toward the cabin. If ya knew Ma, you'd know when someone was ailin', she was in command. Me and Pa just stood back and did what we were told.

One of the advantages of being the last kid left at home is I had my own blankets and the whole loft to myself. That night, as Diver dosed by the kitchen fire, I laid in my sleeping loft, wrapped up in my worn but surprisingly warm blankets, and listened to Ma and Pa talk in their bedroom.

Pa told Ma several stories: There was his hunt for the bear, his visit with Two Hand, and how he saw the man come plunging down the waterfall. There was the rescue of the stranger and giving him the handle of Diver when he couldn't remember his own name. Pa figured anybody that could survive an eighty-foot drop down them falls deserved to be called Diver. Then he told Ma about the arduous trek home and how he came to admire Diver for his uncomplaining nature and pleasant companionship.

Later that night I reviewed Pa's story and did the math. If Pa's day-to-day description of saving Diver, buildin' the travois, and makin' the trek home was correct, he pulled the man from that pool on my birthday.

I don't know why, but in my mind that kinda gave us a connection.

The next several days were mighty rough on Diver. He had developed a fever on the long cold trek home, but he wasn't a complainer by nature, and hadn't mentioned it to Pa. Not that Pa could have done much about it anyway, other than make him some spruce tea, or something to warm up his innards.

Anyway, after three days or so, he'd gotten so bad off that Ma feared we might lose him. Gettin' a bit desperate I suppose, she finally sent Pa down to the Cove to get that new doctor folks had been talkin' about...Doc Kendree.

It was uncommon and strange at our house to be asking for outside help, but then again, having Pa drag home a complete stranger was uncommon and strange in itself.

After examining Diver, the doctor said his broken arm and his sprained knee seemed to be doing good.

Many of the contusions were already fading and the displaced hip, though still mighty painful, was just fine. As for the fever—the most dangerous of Diver's ailments—he figured some bloodletting would be in order. Pa disagreed, which didn't set too well with Doc Kendree. But after seein' the look in Pa's eye, he agreed to a course of castor oil and prayer.

He gave Ma the castor oil and told her the right dosage to induce vomiting. He then said he'd check in on Diver again in a week or so. Pa figured a week or so would be a bit too late if something were to happen, but it really didn't matter anyway. We never saw hide nor hair of the doctor again. I guess Pa scared him off.

Ma tried a dose of castor oil on Diver, but it made him so sick she never tried it again. Instead, she gave him small sips of ginseng root and dogwood bark teas.

A couple nights later his fever broke and come mornin' he was weak as a church mouse, but otherwise, in fine fiddle. He was mighty hungry too.

Ma's fine cookin' worked miracles on Diver. It wasn't long before he was puttin' on weight and fillin' out some. He got to gettin' antsy 'bout bein' cooped up for so long too.

Though Pa helped Diver get seated at the table, where he insisted on helpin' Ma with cuttin' up meats, choppin' vegetables, kneadin' dough, or assisting her with anything else she might could use some help with, he still felt the need to get himself movin' about.

Finally, Pa fashioned a crutch and a cane out of red-cedar branches, and Diver started experimentin' with walkin' about a bit. It didn't take long before he was staggerin' around the homestead just as free as could be. And I think Ma was feeling free too. That's not to say she wasn't thankful for the help he'd given her, but she was just plumb happy to have her kitchen back to herself.

Pa spent most of his time huntin' and trappin' to build-up our supply of winter meat. A chore that had been delayed far too long by the bear hunt and needed takin' care of. In his absence, Diver got in the habit of exploring his surroundings. And I made a habit of going with him when I wasn't prevented by school or chores and such.

One of my chores was choppin' wood, which I didn't care much for. Diver would have been happy to do it, but he couldn't have managed, what with his arm in a splint and all, even if I'd let him try. He did check my snares each day though, and even improved my fishing line by including a funnel-trap.

One Saturday, when we were out explorin', we came across a small cave. It was perhaps a half-mile downstream from the cabin and a couple-hundred yards the other side of the creek. I couldn't believe me and my best friend, Henry Rainwater, an Indian boy who lived on Black Gum Shoal with his mother Long Star, hadn't noticed it before.

I reckon we'd missed it cause the narrow entrance, a six-foot-tall, two-foot-wide gash, was tucked in behind a wall of rhododendrons that clung to a steep slope.

Inside, it opened into a small chamber about twenty-feet-long by ten-feet-wide. It had a crack running along the west side of its twelve-foot ceiling with a thin beam of natural light blazing through giving the chamber a soft glow. A trickle of cold spring water dribbled down the east wall, where it followed a swale in the floor for a few feet before disappearing into another crack.

At the rear of the cave was a level-topped rock

bench. It was about eight-feet-long, nearly three-feet-deep, and stood a couple-feet off the floor. If I didn't know better, I'd have thought it was manmade. How could such a bed-like shelf have formed naturally? It's beyond me.

Even with the fair amount of light streaming through the ceiling crack we couldn't see into the darkest corners too well, so Diver said we'd come back sometime with a torch and get a better look.

During our forays through the countryside, Diver expanded my knowledge of the plants, rocks, and animals, I thought I'd been familiar with my whole life. He was like an endless resource of information on nature. I was amazed to learn how little I really knew.

It was also interesting to see him speak on subjects that he didn't even realize he knew about until they came up. To me, he seemed to know just about everything about everything . . . except his own name.

It wasn't long before Miss Melloncamp overheard me telling some classmates at school about the things Diver had taught me. She decided it would be a good idea to have me, an average student at best, teach the whole class. I think that her great bulk, and her finicky demeanor, prevented her from experiencing nature for herself, beyond what she read, but she still figured it was knowledge that needed to be passed along to the next generation. Maybe it added to her ideal of a "well rounded education," as she called it.

As it so happened, it sure added to my education.

You'd think that freely passing along information, and teaching, and whatnot, would be a good thing. That no one would take offence to it. And you'd be right when it came to the younger kids. Problem was, it didn't set real well with a few of the older boys. Especially Tyrone Beckett and his pals.

Tyrone was a year older than me, and he was the grandson of Jud Beckett, the second richest man in the Cove. Now, Tyrone's Pa, Trace Beckett, was a giant of a man. He was a hard worker, but just about as mean as a man could come. And there was nobody that Trace hated more than my older brother, Forrest.

83

Folks figured part of that hate was jealousy cause Forrest was foreman over all of Trace's Uncle, Orwell Beckett's holdings. Orwell was the wealthiest man in the Cove, perhaps in the entire county. But I believe the main reason for the hatred was that Forrest was a mighty big man also, and he was the only man in the Cove that Trace couldn't buffalo. And, when a man won't cow-tow to a bully, people take notice, especially the bully.

So, you can imagine, here I am, the little brother of the man Tyrone's father hates above all others. And I'm gonna presume to teach Tyrone and his pals? Not likely. Of course, they didn't show their disdain in class. Miss Melloncamp wouldn't have put up with it. But I doubt I'd have noticed it even if they had.

I was gettin' all flustered over Mary Wilson, the preacher's daughter, glancing at me outta the corner of her eye, and giving me a little bashful smile that like to scared me half to death. I didn't know what had brought it on, but it sure riled my innards somethin' fierce.

I was too young to realize, I was plumb smitten.

Lucky for me, Second Chance Fieldman was

paying attention to what was going on.

Second Chance's dad, Chance Sr., was Forrest's best friend and he worked for him on Orwell's farm. Orwell had nine hundred acres in the Cove, and he had three other large holdings throughout the county.

Chance Senior's son, Chance, Jr., was my only real friend at school seein's as how Henry, being an Indian, wasn't allowed to enroll. Already having another Junior in class, Miss Melloncamp chose to call Chance, Jr. by the initials, C.J., but outta school me and Henry called him Second Chance.

Anyway, after school let out that day, while we were all pulling on our coats, scarves, and gloves, getting ready to face a long cold walk home, Second Chance quietly slipped over and trying to be as nonchalant as possible, whispered in my ear.

"What you gonna do?"

I looked at him, not knowing what he was talking about and said, "Do about what?"

"About Tyrone, Jack, and Kenny," he whispered as he half covered his mouth and nodded their way.

I glanced over at the three of them as they quickly slipped out the door, still pulling on their

85

coats and gloves as a cold breeze swept across the bare wood floor.

"I don't know what you're talking about," I said.

The look on Second Chance's face showed sympathy for his dim-witted friend, but I think he sometimes questioned his long-suffering determination to help the clueless.

"While you were busy making googly eyes with Mary Wilson, I heard Tyrone telling Jack and Kenny, they're going to wait for you down by Abrams Creek and teach you a lesson about nature."

I kinda took a defensive stance having my feathers all ruffled up like Ma's big old Leghorn rooster. I said, "I wasn't making googly eyes with Mary Wilson."

Second Chance burst out laughing and said, "That's the part that bothers you? What about Tyrone?"

"Well, I don't know," I said, "but I wasn't making googly eyes."

Second Chance offered to walk down to Abrams Creek with me, but it was cold as the dickens out there and it wasn't on his way home.

"No," I said. "I'll be fine. You go on home, and I'll see ya later."

He seemed a bit reluctant about not backing me up, but also a whole lot relieved. After donning his cap, he gave me a nod and slipped out the door to head home.

Now, you might figure I was in a bit of a fix. And, truth be told, I was. I had no choice but to cross Abrams Creek to get home, and Abrams Creek only had one bridge. In the summertime it wouldn't have been a problem to wade across the creek anywhere that I chose, but being winter, the half-frozen stream was far too cold.

As I stood there pondering, Miss Melloncamp, who had been busy straightening desks and making sure slates and sticks of chalk were properly stored, straightened up and drew in a deep breath. A quite audible gurgle rumbled from her abundant midriff.

She didn't seem to notice as she looked at me and asked, "Did you need something, Billy?"

"No, Miss Melloncamp," I said as I furiously tried to think of a reason to be standing around.

By chance, I noticed the wood pile by the old soot-blackened potbelly stove was gettin' a bit low.

"I just thought I might bring in some kindlin' for ya, if you'd like," I said.

"Well, how thoughtful of you Billy," she replied. "Yes, I would like that very much."

I tightened my scarf around my ears and headed out to the woodpile alongside the little one-room schoolhouse. A light snow had been falling off and on all day, so I had to knock the crust off of each stick as I picked it up. No big deal, but it did burn up a bit of time.

Not far away, stood a small shack the community gave the schoolmarm to use when she wasn't staying with the family of one of her pupils.

It was a common practice at the time for students' parents to take turns housing the teacher throughout the school year.

I thought about it as I gathered up an armful of split hickory. Trudging back around to the front of the schoolhouse and stomping the snow off my shoes before entering, I placed the wood in its place.

"You want me to fetch some wood over to your place too, Miss Melloncamp?" I asked.

"No Billy," she said. "I'm staying at the Cramdon's this week. But thank you. You've been very helpful. Run along home now."

As I turned to leave, she added, "And, have a good weekend."

"I will," I said as I opened the door. "You too."

She was right of course. I had to go home sometime. All I could do was hope Tyrone and his buddies had given up waiting on me.

SEVEN

Billy Goat Gruff

TYRONE AND HIS BUDDIES had not given up. I suppose even frostbite is fair exchange for a good bit of bedevilment.

As I walked down the two-track through a flurry of snowflakes as big as oak leaves, my head was on a swivel. I knew my tormentors were out there, I just didn't know where.

When I reached the slope leading down to the Abrams Creek Bridge, I stopped to survey the way ahead. Nothing was in view except Mr. Nolman's old hay wagon, and that had been sitting in the field with a broken rear axle since last July. I couldn't believe it. *Had they gone home after all?*

I almost felt disappointed as I hurried on down to the bridge. My mind conjured up what would have happened if they'd stuck around. I'd have had to defend myself of course. Who could blame me for that? And I reckon some of those boys may have gotten hurt. Not that I'd have taken pleasure in it, you understand, but me being my father's son, I just may not have been able to hold myself back.

With my mind so consumed by daydreams of glory and splendor, I didn't notice Jack and Kenny peek over the sideboards of Mr. Nolman's wagon. They waited until I was just stepping onto the bridge before jumping out and rushing up behind me. Hearin' their shoes slapping on the frozen ground, I spun around.

"Gotcha now, Billy," Jack shouted.

I could see that Kenny wasn't as thrilled about this whole thing as Jack was. To tell the truth, he'd always seemed like a decent kid to me. But we both knew he couldn't back down now. Where Tyrone and Jack led, he would follow.

As I backed onto the bridge, keeping an eye on the two boys, it struck me. Where was Tyrone?

Then, from behind, I heard, "Now, what you gonna do, Billy boy? You never should o' stepped on my bridge. Maybe I'll call ya Billy Goat Gruff."

I spun around and saw Tyrone climbing onto the planking from his hiding place beneath the off ramp.

"This big bad troll has done caught you on his bridge, and he's going to eat you all up," he said.

I could hear Jack laughing behind me. "You is a mean old troll, Tyrone," he said. "Show him what you do when a Billy Goat crosses your bridge."

It's pretty amazing how quickly daydream bravado fades when you're facing the danger in real life. I didn't embarrass myself by wetting my drawers or anything like that, but truth be told, I wasn't far from it.

"What do ya want, Tyrone?" I stammered. "I ain't done nothing to you."

"Oh, you ain't done nothing to me?" he sneered. "Well now, didn't I just catch ya crossin' my bridge."

He leered over at Jack. "Didn't I just catch him crossin' my bridge?"

"You sure did," said Jack. "He was just strollin' along like *he* was the owner of your bridge."

Tyrone looked at me. "What you say about that, Billy Goat?"

92

"No. . . no . . . nobody owns this bridge." I stuttered.

"Ha!" laughed Tyrone. "We'll see about that."

Jack and Kenny started closing in on me from behind while Tyrone did the same from in front.

I didn't know what to do. I couldn't take on Jack and Kenny; not together anyway. But did I have a chance of getting past Tyrone?

Maybe I should jump off the bridge and try for shore, I thought. *It would be a cold walk home, but better than a black eye or missing tooth.*

None of the options sounded all that great, but I sure didn't want to see what Tyrone would do to a goat on his bridge.

I'd about made up my mind to jump when I heard a voice from heaven. In reality, it was Diver. But it sure sounded like an angel to me.

"Hey there Billy," he called. "You're running a bit late from school today. I thought I'd come walk with ya for a ways."

"Yeah," I said, feelin' my heart rate begin to slow and the blood return to my extremities. "I was just tellin' my pals here I ain't got time to teach 'em any more today. I got chores to do, and Ma's probably got supper waitin'."

I could see the anger flair in Tyrone's eyes as I slipped past him.

"This ain't the end of it," he hissed in a voice only I could hear.

I'd like to say I had a snappy comeback, but in all truth, nothing came to mind. Even if it had, I'm not sure my dry mouth could've spoken it.

The sixth day of January, what some folks call Old Christmas, turned out to be a very special day for the Banion Clan that year.

Diver had been spending more and more time roaming 'round both the countryside, and the Cove itself. It was not unusual for me to hurriedly dress in the early morning chill, climb down from my loft on the way to the necessity, and notice that Diver was already gone.

Oftentimes, he wouldn't return till well after dark; half-frozen and tired to the bone, yet always with that good-natured attitude he wrapped himself in like a cloak. If we asked where he'd been, he'd say, "Oh, here and there. Just enjoyin' the good day that the Lord has made."

That kinda answer would plumb shut your mouth cause how ya gonna question it.

Ma would simply say, "That's nice," and continue on with whatever chore she happened to be doin' at the moment.

Of course, we knew she was about ready to pop with curiosity. You see, Ma spent so much time there at the homestead doing the cooking, cleaning, gardening, and whatnot, that her need for adventure was largely fulfilled through tales that others told of their daily exploits. Like when Pa would come in from one of his extended hunting trips or fur selling ventures. Why, Ma's eyes would plumb shine as she waited to hear every detail of his journey.

Well, anyway, it was after one of those long days of roaming that Diver came in and sat at the table where we sat eatin' a late supper. As Ma got up to fix him a plate and cut a couple more slices of fresh bread, he began to talk. At first it was just this, that and the other. Nothing of any import. But before long

95

you could feel he was workin' his way around to sayin' what he'd come to say. I guess he just didn't know how to bring the subject up.

I glanced at Pa, and he gave me a wink. Surprised me so bad milk spewed from my nose. Luckily, I don't think anyone noticed.

After lettin' Diver flounder for a while, Pa finally took pity on him and slapped his big hand on the table.

"If you're gonna be sayin' somethin', Diver," he said, "I sure wish you'd get to it. It's gettin' downright uncomfortable watchin' you squirm about like ol' Billy here that day he threw a rock at a beehive."

I remember that day well. I don't recommend it.

"Well, ya see, what it is, is, I'm needin' your help," said Diver. "You, Kate, and Billy, too."

Pa looked him straight in the eye and grinned.

"Why, that ain't no reason to be actin' like a blushin' bride after a bean and onion dinner."

Ma covered her mouth and actually did blush.

Diver grinned back and said, "You ain't heard what I'm askin' yet."

He then looked around the table and said, "I'm

needing y'all to do what I ask, and not ask any questions."

He looked at Ma. "I know this is especially hard on you Kate, but it will be well worth it. I promise."

We all sat there rather perplexed for a moment.

"Okay," said Pa. "I don't know what all the mystery is, but if you're needin' somethin', you know all you gotta do is ask."

"And you're sayin' you'll do it, no questions asked?" repeated Diver.

"That's what I said," said Pa looking a bit more suspicious.

"Good," said Diver. "Come Saturday, I need y'all to dress in your very best and be prepared to go somewhere with me at around ten in the mornin'. I done took care of the transportation so don't fret none about that."

"What's this all about?" asked Pa.

Me and Ma didn't know what to think.

"Now Zeb," said Diver. "You done said you'd do as I asked, no questions. I'm gonna hold you to that."

Pa shook his head as if he'd been hornswoggled.

"I'm thinking I'd've been better off goin' after that

bear," he muttered. "Least ways, it wouldn't be askin' no favors."

Diver laughed as he left the table.

"I'll be back directly," he said as he headed out the back door.

I saw wonder glowing in Ma's eyes. She suddenly grabbed Pa's hand and said, "You don't think he's gettin' married, do you?"

"Married?" cried Pa. "What brought that on?"

"Well, you know as well as I do how he's been takin' off and not comin' home 'till the wee hours of the mornin'," Ma said. "Where could he be goin'? I think he's been meetin' up with someone."

"Hogwash," said Pa, droppin' his fork into his empty plate and commencin' to pick at a huckleberry thorn embedded in his left wrist.

It seemed to be an outlandish notion, but as Ma sat there watchin' Pa's face, she could see the doubt begin to furrow his brow. She knew good and well she'd got him to thinkin'. Smiling to herself, she motioned for me to help and began gathering up the dishes and leftovers. Saturday just couldn't come soon enough to her way of thinkin'.

The only thing Ma liked better than a mystery, was gettin' to the bottom of a mystery.

≈

We were sittin' at the kitchen table midmorning on Saturday when we heard a jangling out front.

"Sounds like he's here," Diver said as he used his good hand to help steady himself when he rose from the table. He grabbed his coat, then headed for the door.

Ma and Pa glanced at each other, then bundled up and followed suit with me close behind.

A cold breeze greeted us as we left the warm cabin and stood staring across the front yard. There, wrapped in a knee-length, dyed wool overcoat, stood Forrest. Behind him was the most magnificent horse and coach I'd ever seen.

Forrest hurried across the snowy yard, lifted Ma into his massive arms, and swung her around as he kissed her cheek.

She laughed like a schoolgirl.

"Oh, Forrest," she giggled. "Put me down before ya squish out my innards."

He smiled that five-dollar smile of his, and Ma kissed him back before he set her down.

"I'm mighty glad to see you, Ma," Forrest said. "For sure, you're still the prettiest gal I ever laid eyes on."

"Oh, hooey," said Ma kinda gettin' a little red around the gills. "You always were the smoothest talkin' child I ever seen."

Forrest's grin slipped some when he reached out to shake Pa's hand.

"Pa," he said.

"Forrest," Pa replied.

Some folks reckoned that Pa and Forrest had a bit of a feud goin', but that ain't rightly so. I reckon the discomfort between them started when Forrest decided it was time for him to get out and make his own way in the world. He moved down to the Cove and went to work for Orwell Beckett, which Pa couldn't understand, seein's how he himself had never worked for another man in his adult life. At the same time, Forrest felt like Pa was trying to hold onto a way of life whose time had run its course. There was no real animosity between the two, they'd simply grown apart. Figured they had nothing in common. Each to his own.

"Quite a rig there, isn't it," Diver said to Pa, trying to start a dialog.

"Sure is," said Pa as he walked over to inspect it.

His hand slid along the glossy black paint of the handsome coach before patting the stuffed leather seats on his way to admire the stunning Belgian horse decked out in silver studded tack. Though Pa was a mule man at heart, he always had appreciated the beauty of a well-cared-for carriage horse.

"Where'd ya get it?" he asked as Forrest walked up with Ma on his right arm and his ham-sized left hand resting on my shoulder.

"Belongs to Orwell Beckett," said Forrest. "When he made me his foreman, he said I could use it when I liked. Up to now, I never had cause."

"Yep, quite a set-up," said Pa.

"Reckon we best get to going," said Forrest.

He helped Ma up into the backseat and Pa followed. Diver and myself both climbed up front. As Forrest walked around to the back of the carriage, he opened a wood and brass trunk and withdrew a couple thick wool blankets. He handed one to Pa, and one to me and Diver. He then climbed aboard and wrapped a third one that was already on the front seat around his large frame. Once settled in, he placed his foot on the dashboard and taking the reins from the handbrake, flicked his wrist. The magnificent Belgian eased into the trace lines and began plodding along.

I can't say when I've ever had a more enjoyable ride. The clop-clop-clop of the Belgian's iron shoes ringing over the frozen snowscape. The trees and bushes sparkling with a million tiny icicles. The sight of a big-bodied whitetail buck trotting across the remnants of a snowy cornfield. They all seemed to vie for the right to grace a master painter's palette. It was a scene I don't reckon I'll ever forget. Especially, how that big old buck stopped and stood there watching as we disappear behind a row of towering pine trees. It was a magical journey.

When we reached the bridge over Abrams Creek, the hoof beats changed in timbre from clip-clop to clump-clump as the rough-hewn boards clattered under the weight of the horse and the grind of iron rimmed wheels. Diver and I glanced at each other and smiled. We'd not told anyone about Billy Goat Gruff or Diver's assist in my escape from the local bullies.

Before long we pulled into a circle drive in front of Forrest's house. Good to their word, during the entire trip, Ma and Pa had not asked where we were going... or why.

Forrest and Sarah May's home was quite impressive by Cove standards. It was a two-story clapboard dwelling, painted white, with black shutters gracing its double hung windows. Two windows were on the ground level in front, with four across the face of the second story. The rear of the structure was opposite with two above and four below. An elegant, oversized door with a brass ringer sat below a portico at the center of the circle driveway. Two large stone chimneys bracketed each end of the house, towering above the shake-shingle roof.

Out back was the necessity to the left, and a root cellar and tool shed to the right. Near the rear porch, for easy access, was a peak roofed, spring water wellhouse.

All along the foundation of the house was planted

a variety of bushes found in the Cove area, and though covered by snow this time of year, the back yard was home to a large vegetable garden.

No sooner did Forrest ease the carriage to a stop than the front door flew open, and Sarah May beckoned us all to come in.

I climbed down as Pa helped Ma.

"Y'all go on in," said Forrest. "Me and Diver are gonna put up the horse and we'll be right along."

As we headed for the house, Forrest pulled back out onto the hard-packed road and headed for a barn I could see about a quarter mile down the road.

I didn't know how Diver had managed to arrange what he had, but it sure looked to be the makings of a special day.

EIGHT

Dinner

A S WE ENTERED THE HOUSE, Sarah May said, "Welcome, welcome. I'm so glad you could come for Old Christmas dinner."

Ma and Pa both hugged Sarah amidst a gaggle of excited, laughing children.

"Kids, settle down," Sarah May said as she took each child by the shoulder and lined them up in front of their grandparents.

Ma stooped down and clutched the three giggling kids with both arms. "Who you got here Sarah May? This can't be yourn and Forrest's bunch. Why, last time I saw them they were just wee little sprouts. These here are near growed."

"You know it's me," laughed Darlene as she wiggled outta Ma's grasp. "And this is Wes," she said tapping Forrest Weston on the head.

"And I'm Anny Lynn," the youngest shouted before Darlene could introduce her.

"Well, I'll be," said Ma with an exaggerated shake of her head. "Can you believe it Grandpa? Our precious little tadpoles are 'bout too big to be needin' hugs and kisses from the likes of us old folks."

"We'll always be needing you Grandma. You too Grandpa," said Darlene. The other kids stood nodding their heads and smiling.

Ma stood and took Pa's arm with a smile on her face and a glow in her eyes.

"And how are you doing Billy," Sarah May said giving me a hug.

I felt like the tips of my ears were gonna catch fire. If I could of seen myself, I figure I was about as red as a holly berry. That Sarah May was about the prettiest lady I'd ever seen, and to tell the truth, I'd had a crush on her for as long as I could remember. I think I muttered somethin' about doing just fine, but I ain't real sure.

The kids settled down a bit and came over to greet me too.

Sarah May then looked up at Pa and said, "There's somebody else that wants to say hi."

She nodded at the kitchen doorway.

There stood Delma and James, smilin' to beat the band.

"Delma," cried Pa as he rushed over to grab her.

"Papa," she shouted with outstretched arms.

For the second time in my life, I saw a tear in Pa's eye. This time it rolled right on down his cheek, and I don't think he even took notice.

While all this was going on, Forrest and Diver came in and were enjoying the show.

"How?" said Pa. "When? I mean, what are you doing here."

"It was Diver and Sarah May," said Delma. "Sarah wrote me and told me all about your great bear hunt, and how you brought Diver home, and how she and Diver had become such close friends and decided to have an Old Christmas dinner for the whole family. And how it just wouldn't be right if me and James weren't here..."

She had to stop to catch her breath.

"Well, of course we came," she continued. "You

couldn't have kept us away if you'd set that killer bear on us."

Everyone was smiling and laughing by then.

Then Delma turned and hugged Ma.

"Oh, Ma, I've missed you so much," she said.

"I know, baby," Ma said. "It's been much too long."

As she hugged Delma, she reached out and squeezed James' hand.

"Why don't you boys go on into the parlor," said Sarah May. "Let us ladies get dinner done."

Ma had to smile at the word "parlor". *Can you imagine a Banion owning a parlor?* she thought.

Fact is, the whole house was a marvel.

When Forrest had first become Orwell's foreman and was presented with the new house, Sarah had given Ma a tour. It had four bedrooms upstairs and one down. On the ground floor was also a parlor and front foyer, a spacious kitchen, and even a separate dining room.

The kitchen was Ma's favorite room. It had a full cooking fireplace with cast iron equipment, along with a separate wood burning cook stove which made life so much easier. There was a dry sink, butcher-block worktable, storage cabinets, and a beautiful pie pantry with a wheat pattern punched into the tin door inserts. But perhaps the most luxurious item was the double doors in the south wall which opened up to reveal an honest to goodness brass tub. It even had a plug that drained right out into the yard.

As Ma, Sarah, Delma and seven-year-old Darlene went to work with a steady stream of chattering and gossip flowing from the kitchen, us men settled in the Parlor.

Wes and Anny had run off to play in their room.

As Pa and Diver listened to James talk about the advantages of big city life up in Maryville, Forrest worried the fire with a heavy cast iron poker before adding a log and replacing the tool next a small black shovel, brush, and ash bucket. He then opened an innately carved, black walnut cabinet, and removed a crystal pitcher.

"I got me some fine corn liquor here if anyone would care for a sip," he said.

James and Diver both looked at Pa.

Not being a drinking man, yet not wanting to

discourage the others if they cared to partake, he said, "Fine. I reckon I might could handle a sip, being a special occasion and all."

He took the small glass Forrest handed him.

James smiled and said, "Don't mind if I do."

He rose to take the proffered glass and made a show of appraising the contents. He then took a stout nip. Tears edged his eyelids.

"Nice," he said with a catch in his throat. "Smooth as buttermilk."

Diver said, "Thank you," took his glass, and sat it down on the little table next to his chair.

As for me, none was offered or expected.

Time passed pleasantly. For Forrest and James, Pa and Diver retold the tale about Pa's great bear hunt, Diver's fall down the cascade which inspired his name, and the long travois trek home through the wilderness.

James allowed how that was one more advantage to big city life. "No wild beasts tryin' to eat ya. Yep," he said, "There just ain't much more a modern man could possibly want."

Finally, answering an occasional question from Pa

or Diver, Forrest talked about the various crops raised on Orwell's farm and the prospects for the coming year. He downplayed his own role in the undertakings, but it was well known throughout the Cove. Since Forrest had become foreman, Orwell's fortunes had preponderantly increased.

"Yep, that's the Banions for ya," said Diver. "Can't be bested but don't care a lick for the credit. I'd've knowed you were father and son if I'd never laid eyes on ya. Just by the telling. And folks here in the Cove feel the same way. Heard it for myself."

Pa and Forrest were both startled by that remark.

"What you talkin' about, Diver?" said Forrest. "Other than size, maybe, I don't figure there's a whole lot the same about us."

Pa nodded.

"Oh nonsense!" said Diver. "Look at Zeb sittin' there. Ain't a man in these mountains that would challenge him to a one on one when it comes to hunting, trapping, and just plain ol' surviving in these hills."

Pa kinda shifted 'round in his chair. He'd never been comfortable being talked about in such a way.

Knowin' his own compass was good enough for him.

"And then you," Diver continued. "Ain't nobody can handle a gang of field hands, or figure what crops hold the best prospects for what year, or even when's the prime time to harvest to bring in top dollar the way you do. I'm telling ya, you two are your own men. If it's being done, ain't no one gonna do it better. Why, if you two were to swap lifestyles, ain't a body in the Cove would take notice."

Pa and Forrest both pondered on that for a while. Neither had ever considered they may be alike in any way. Pa, the hunter. Forrest, the farmer. What could be more opposite? But Diver's take did make sense. Maybe they were more alike than they realized.

Shortly after Diver's observation, Sarah May came to the parlor door and called us for dinner.

When we entered the dining room, I reckon I laid eyes on the most magnificent bird I'd ever seen. In the center of the heavy oak table, on a silver platter, rested an enormous beautiful golden-brown turkey. Stretched along a linen runner from the head to toe of the table sat bowls of mashed potatoes, stuffing, ramps, string beans, and tri-colored Indian corn.

112

Also, biscuits, clover honey with the comb, and about two pounds of fresh churned butter. To drink, we had fresh sweet milk, buttermilk, sassafras tea, and dandelion wine.

"My word," exclaimed Pa as he entered the room. "I ain't seen nothin' like this since I was invited to a shindig down in New Orleans to honor Andy Jackson himself."

The gals were beaming, Darlene nearly jumping with joy. Her hands were clasped together, and I think I heard a little squeal escape her big toothed smile.

Forrest moved to take the head of the table, and Sarah motioned for Pa to take the toe. Then the rest of us piled in; all but the three kids who had their own small table.

As we eyed the feast, Pa looked at Forrest. "That's a mighty fine bird," he said.

"Yes sir, it sure is," said Forest. "But I can't take the credit."

Pa said, "That right?" a bit puzzled.

Diver spoke up then. "No, Zeb, we're all gonna be feasting like kings today thanks to Billy here." He reached over and patted me on the back.

I like to choked where I sat. I'd never laid eyes on the bird before.

"Billy?" said Pa looking at me.

"That's right," said Diver. "That bird came from Billy's own snare line."

"Well, I'll be," said Pa. Then looking at Forrest, he said, "Looks like you and me got some competition for being Banion of the hill."

I don't think you could have fit my head in a fifty-gallon barrel.

I was sitting there with everybody lookin' and smilin' at me, and didn't know what to say. I could feel my face gettin' redder and redder, so I finally mumbled, "Aw, shucks, Diver. Why don't you ask grace, and let's eat the thing?"

Everybody laughed and we all settled down to a wonderful meal.

After dinner we all sat around enjoying each other's company until Sarah May said we had just a couple more surprises coming. First, Forrest went out to bring in a huge bowl of black raspberry ice cream.

No one there, outside of Forrest's family, had ever had ice cream, and it was a big hit. I reckon Pa may have burst if it hadn't run out. I was kinda tickled 'bout the dribbles of cream in his whiskers before Ma came over and wiped it out for him.

Then Sarah May said, "And now, Delma's got something for us."

We all looked at Delma as she walked over to Ma and Pa. They stood up. With a smile as big as a harvest moon, she took their hands in each of hers and said, "Mama, Papa, we're gonna have a baby!"

Ma screamed and hugged Delma while Pa stood there staring as if in shock. Finally, Pa gave a "Whoop!" and grabbed Delma and swung her around as she laughed.

Suddenly, he stopped and put her down. With a concerned look on his face he said, "I'm sorry. Are you all right?"

Everybody laughed together as she said, "I'm perfect, *Grandpa*."

That night after Forrest dropped us off at our cabin, Pa laid his big ol' hand on Diver's shoulder.

"Thank you, Diver," he said. "It feels like my whole family's been restored to me, and I owe it all to you."

"No thanks needed, my friend," Diver replied. "They've been here all along."

NINE

A Reward For Diver

THE MORNING AFTER the Banion family get together, Diver sat at the kitchen table as me and Ma washed the breakfast dishes. He was scratching and pawing at his splinted arm while Pa sat against the far wall cleaning his flintlock.

"Kate," Diver said, "What do you say, will ya help me take this thing off?"

She glanced over her shoulder. "Think it's been on long enough, do ya?"

"Yeah," he said, flexing his bum hand. "The way I see it, we get rid of this torture device today, or I'm gonna cut the whole arm off, in which case what was the point in the first place?"

Pa grinned as he rammed his cleaning rod down

the barrel one last time.

Ma said, "Well, I sure don't want ya to cut your arm off. I'd be left to clean up the mess. Let's get at it."

After removing the wrapped splint boards, she carefully stripped back several feet of cloth strips. In moments the tender flesh beneath was exposed for the first time since the accident.

"Ahh," Diver said. "That's better. I'm not thinkin' I'll be missing that thing any time soon."

He held up his newly freed arm next to the good one. Thin and white, it looked downright strange. Kinda like an underfed, albino king snake next to its dairy barn reared cousin. Diver stood there staring at it, not knowing what to say.

Ma could see the look of despair on his face.

"No need to be feeling like a three-legged coonhound," she said. "I happen to know a thing or two about perkin' up a puny arm. Why, my miraculous method ain't never failed. No time at all, you'll be struttin' around like a banty rooster in a three-story chicken coop."

"That sounds great Kate," he said, wide-eyed and all. "What do I do?"

"See that basket over there?" Ma said.

Diver glanced at the woven reed basket.

"Yeah," he uttered.

"It's full of laundry," Ma said. "Get t' washin'."

Diver grinned and shook his head, "I should've known," he said.

Ma laughed, "I said it'd perk that arm up and I wasn't lyin'."

Pa, replacing the newly oiled lock on his rifle, sat back and listened as Ma teased Diver. He grinned and began whistling the Colonial Army's retreat ditty.

I laughed.

Fact is, Ma was right. In no time at all Diver's arm was fairin' real fine. It wasn't long after that, that Diver asked Pa if he would mind a little construction going on around the place.

"What ya got in mind?" asked Pa.

"Well, Zeb," he said. "I reckon you may have noticed I been moseying off now and again, and coming in at strange hours and all?"

"Didn't hafta notice," Pa said. "Got Kathryn doin' it for me."

Diver scratched his chin and let that sit a spell.

118

"Yep. Guess you got a pretty good handle on things at that." He took a quick look around and said, "But don't be tellin' Kate I said such a thing."

Pa gave a little wink and grinned.

"Anyway," said Diver. "As you know, I've been spendin' some time down in the Cove. Got to know Forrest and Sarah May pretty well. Then, of course, Forrest introduced me to Orwell Beckett. Orwell mentioned how highly he thought of you for going after that bear that killed young Joey Cobb. Well, that got us to talkin' 'bout the Cobbs and how poorly Abner Cobb was fairin' cause that hog-bit leg of his'n took to festerin' some. Seems all Doc Kendree wanted to do was bleed him and feed him castor oil."

Pa gritted his teeth. "I've seen enough men die from bleedin' out to know it's better to keep the stuff inside your body, no matter what some highfalutin' quack says," he grumbled. "General Washington may have been around a heap longer if they'd let him be."

"Can't say it no truer," said Diver. "Anyway, after we talked for a bit, Orwell lets out that Kendree told the Cobb's neighbors they oughta stay away from their house cause o' bad humors."

"Likely wanted somethin' to blame his own incompetence on," said Pa.

"By that time," Diver continued, "me and Forrest were both 'bout fit to be tied. I figured I'd go give the Cobbs a visit myself to see if they could use a little comfortin' or whatnot."

He hung his head and sighed.

"When I knocked, Millie answered the door. I'm tellin' ya, Zeb," his Adam's apple bobbed as he swallowed, "that poor woman done looked like death itself. And the smell! Well, you been on battlefields . . . no need to tell *you* what it's like."

He snatched the hat off his head and slapped it against his leg. He was in pain just thinkin' about it.

"Well, I explained who I was and said I'd come by to see if I could be of help. It was tough, Zeb. Her eyes welled up in disbelief and gratitude as she sniffled into a scented hanky. Hesitantly, she nodded and stepped outta the way."

Diver had a blank stare for a moment before replacing his hat. He then continued.

"It was bad, Zeb. When I stepped into that house . . . it was real bad. Abner was layin' on a cot against the back wall, and I could smell the scent of rot plum across the room. I walked over and his bare leg was in an awful mess. The pig had got him just below the knee. The wound was all swollen and black, and like I said, it smelled somethin' fierce.

"I figured blood poisonin' had set-in and there probably wasn't a thing could be done for it. I laid my hand on his forehead, and it was like pickin' up a glowin' ember from the fire,"

"So, what'd you do?" asked Pa.

"I couldn't let him suffer like that," Diver stated, "so I had Millie holler for Ben. You remember that boy that came to help out?"

"Yeah, I met him up on Gregory Bald," Pa said.

"Anyway," continued Diver, "I told Ben to take Millie to a neighbor's house 'cause I didn't want her to see what needed to be done. I also told him to have somebody run over and get some ginseng root from Sarah May. She keeps a pound or two stored for medicinal purposes same as Kate does. On the way back, I said for him to snatch some bark off that dogwood tree by the church and get back here as quickly as possible. I figured if Kate's tea worked for my fever, it might help Abner's.

"Ben didn't look real happy 'bout comin' back, and truth be told, I can't say I blame him. While he was gone, I made a mixture of bread, milk, and salt for a poultice and wrapped it in a clean rag. I then put the paste in a tin bowl with a little water to heat by the fire. Looking around a bit, I found a good sharp knife I figured would do the job. By the time Ben got back, I was ready."

Pa kinda grimaced, knowing what was coming.

"I told Ben it wasn't gonna be pretty, but we had to get the pus outta Abner's leg before it turned to poison and killed him. At the moment Abner was out, but I knew that wouldn't last long. Once I went to pokin' around, he'd be climbin' the walls. I told Ben I needed him to lay across his uncle's chest and hold him down. He looked a might green, but it stands to show what that youth is made of. He stilled himself and said he was game."

Pa's opinion of Ben took a couple notches up.

"I placed a bucket under the bed to catch the mess," Diver said, "then had Ben tie Abner's leg down to the rail right above the knee and at the ankle. I'll tell ya, I was prayin' somebody else would come walkin' through the door and take over, but I knew that wasn't gonna happen. There was nothing for it. It had to be done. I took the knife in my good hand and slid the tip straight down into that mound of putrid flesh on one side of the wound. Abner like to throwed that boy plumb across the room."

"'Grab him!', I shouted.

"Ben jumped right back in there. I gotta say, that young man's got sand. Anyway, when I looked at the cut there wasn't but a trickle of thick black pus oozing from the wound. Not near enough to do the job.

"But the stench! Me and Ben were both gagging and trying not to breathe through our noses.

"Unfortunately, I had no choice but to grab the abscess and squeeze the filth out.

"Abner gave a gargled groan, and thankfully passed out.

"I squeezed as hard as I could. Even used my bad hand. At first little happened. Then, just as I thought I was going to have to cut him again, the mass popped. A mess of green-black pus came flooding out and ran down into the bucket. Oh man, did that stink. But I was thrilled it was flowing and kept working at it 'til I got everything out that I could. Of course, I still had the other side of the wound to drain. Luckily, it went easier.

"When most everything was out, I placed the warm poultice on the wound to try and draw out the rest of the poison and rushed the bucket outside. You ain't never seen two fellas happier to get into the fresh cold air."

Pa could see the discomfort in his friend's eyes, him reliving the moment as he told it.

"Diver, that's a mighty hard thing you did there," Pa said.

"It wasn't a pleasant task, for sure," Diver said. "But that quack Kendree wasn't gonna do it."

Pa nodded in agreement.

"Anyway, Millie came back, and I showed her how to make the poultice. Told her to apply it for twenty minutes, three or four times a day. Then I made the ginseng-dogwood tea and told her to give Abner small sips of it to help bring the fever down. I also warned her that this might not be enough to save Abner, but I'd be back to check on them every day.

"You can imagine how thrilled I was that I never had to re-drain that wound. Within a week or so, Abner was up and about."

"That's quite a story," said Pa. "But what's it got to do with construction?"

"Well, once Abner got to gettin' around, they wanted to pay me for what I'd done, but they didn't have any money. I told em it wasn't necessary. I didn't do it for compensation. But they wouldn't hear it. Finally, Millie told me to take their nanny goat. Of course, I told them I wasn't gonna do it, but they swore they'd only had the goat for Joey. He was the only one in the house that drank goat's milk. In fact, they claimed that now that he was gone, I'd be doin' em a favor by taking the thing off their hands. Said they wouldn't have to feed it.

"You know, they're proud people, and I could see the need in their eyes to pay the debt they felt they owed. So, I said, 'I sure do like goat's milk. It just seems like an awful high payment for what little I did.' That seemed to please em something fierce. They said to come get the goat as soon as it was convenient."

"So, you're lookin' to build a goat shed?" asked Pa.

"Well, that was the original plan," said Diver. "I figured Kate might like some goat milk. But somehow,

word got around, and I guess Mr. Grear got to feelin'
bad that he hadn't done more for the Cobbs, so he gave
them a Jersey cow, and me one too! Of course, I tried to
turn it down, but he insisted. Now I got a goat and a
cow.

Pa laughed. "You ain't careful, we're gonna be in the
dairy business."

They stood looking at the various structures on the
homestead.

"So, where you figurin' to build?" asked Pa.

"See that flat area, just the other side of the creek?"
Diver asked. "I'd say it's high enough not to flood and
it's got a couple cleared acres that could be fenced for a
pasture. Critters could get to water and have plenty of
grass in the summer. Build a more substantial bridge
across the creek and it wouldn't be all that far from the
house. What do you think?"

"I think you're bitin' off a mighty big chunk, but if
that's your plan, let's do it."

Diver crossed the single-log foot bridge and started
laying out the building site.

Pa headed for his tanning shed to work some green
hides.

TEN

Barns & Butterflies

P A, STANDING ON THE front stoop drinking his coffee, listened as a farm wagon climbed the rise. Not expecting visitors, he idly wondered who it could be.

After several minutes of clacking and creaking the dusty conveyance entered the yard. With a "Whoa," and the clap of the hand brake setting, Forrest climbed down.

"Yo, Forrest," Pa called. "What brings you to the wilds this fine mornin'?"

"Hey, Pa," Forrest returned, walking across the yard. "I'm here on business. Orwell wanted to know if you could help us out?"

Pa eyed him kinda suspicious like. "How's that?"

"Well, we been havin' trouble with hogs rootin' in

127

our winter wheat fields. In fact, I got me a litter of four piglets here in the back of the wagon. Chance's dogs run down their mother and these here survived. We were hopin' you'd take 'em off our hands. Also, Orwell says you can have all the hogs you can kill off his place, if ya want em."

Pa took a sip of coffee and considered the offer.

"Chance has that Bluetick he calls Blue Boy and a Redbone he calls Ricket," Forest continued. "Says you can borrow em anytime you like."

"Yeah, I know Blue Boy and Ricket," Pa said. "They just may be the finest hounds in the mountains. I'll let you know about the pig shootin'. As far as the piglets go, you'll hafta talk to Diver. He seems to be the wrangler 'round here."

Pa turned and spotted Diver stepping off a future fence row.

"Yo, Diver!" he yelled waving his tricorn over his head.

After a moment, Diver noticed and waved back.

"Come on over here," Pa motioned.

It didn't take long for Diver to cross the new bridge we'd built across the creek.

128

"What ya need Zeb?" he asked.

"Ain't my needin', it's Forrest here."

Diver looked at Forrest.

"Ya see, Diver," Forrest began. "I got these piglets here we need to be rid of. I was hopin' you could take 'em off our hands."

As he talked, he threw back an old blanket to reveal four skinny piglets sleeping in a straw lined reed basket.

"Well, I'll be," said Diver, as he looked at the little, white and pink siblings. Looking up, he saw Ma standing at the cabin door. "Kate, come take a look at this, would ya?"

Ma came out, and after giving Forrest a kiss on the cheek, looked in the basket.

"My word," she said. Reaching in, she picked up one of the suddenly squealing little sacks of squirming energy. "Where'd you come from?"

Diver, figuring the piglet was too young to answer for himself, spoke up for it. "Forrest was hopin' we'd take em off his hands. I reckon we could manage it if you don't mind givin' up some of the goat milk. That is, if I get that barn built so we have a goat."

"Looks like you need to be building a pigsty first," Ma said. She turned back toward the house with the piglet settled down and held against her bosom. "I think this little guy is gonna come visit with me for a while."

As she walked away, she glanced back to say, "Good seein' ya, Forrest," then disappeared indoors.

Forrest, grinning, looked at Pa and Diver and said, "I think I just played second fiddle to a pig."

"Yeah," Pa said, "And I think we just got us three eatin' porkers and one pet."

Diver nodded. "Reckon I better be gettin' started on a pigsty and goat shed. The cow barn will have to wait till Saturday."

Squeezing Forrest's arm, he said, "I'm thankin' ya for the critters. Mind if I get a ride when ya head back to the Cove?"

"You got it, Diver," Forrest said. "I'm gonna talk with Pa here for a bit, then I'll be over to help ya out."

As Forrest and Pa watched Diver cross his new bridge and start looking through his pre-cut timbers, Forrest said, "That there is one fine fella."

"Yes, he is," said Pa. "Next to you and Two Hand,

I reckon he's the finest man I've ever known."

Forrest didn't say anything, but he was mighty welled up inside. Praise from Pa was not taken lightly. It felt good.

After the pigsty and temporary goat shed where built, Ma made the men a fine lunch and sat talkin' with em as they ate. The piglet, swollen on sweet milk, slept on her lap. It squirmed around a bit and let drool dampen her apron, but she didn't seem to mind.

When the meal was done and good-byes said, Forrest hauled Diver down to the Cobb's place to get the goat. He offered to drive him back home, but Diver said, "I'm thankin' ya for the offer but I'm lookin' to visit a spell. 'Sides that, it's a mighty fine day for a stroll."

"Well, you take it easy," said Forrest. "I'll see ya on Saturday."

Forrest's duties for Orwell were rather slim in the winter, so he had told Diver he'd help him with the barn on Saturday.

≈

Saturday morning turned out to be unusually warm and sunny for early February. It was the kinda day that makes a man want to get out and get somethin' done.

Ma was busy feeding the piglets a breakfast of goat's milk as Pa watched. Seemed to him, she was wearing more milk than the pigs had managed to swallow. Each time a piglet snorted and chomped his jowls, Ma ended up with more spew on her face or apron.

Pa laughed.

"Oh, shush," said Ma. "You done had your breakfast. Go on and get with ya."

Pa and Diver went out front to talk about the day ahead. Gesturing toward the far streambank, Diver described how in a day or two he figured on havin' a lean-to built to house the new stock.

"May not be the most hansom shelter in the region," he allowed, "but it oughta do the job."

Slowly, the morning stillness was interrupted by an awful racket coming from down the Cove trail. Not a common occurrence on your average early morning

Saturday at the Cove. They stood watching as the clammer grew nearer. The clanging and rattling of wagons couldn't override hearty laughter and boisterous voices as they drifted through the trees.

"What you reckon all the hullabaloo is about?" asked Pa.

"You got me," said Diver. "Sounds like they're fixin' to have a social or a hangin'." He scratched behind his right ear. "Sure, hope it ain't no hangin'."

As they watched, wagons began emerging from around the bend on the final rise to Pa's homestead. There were five in all, and they slowly spread out, parking on the front lawn.

Jumping down from the first wagon, Forrest shouted, "Howdy, Pa! Mighty fine mornin' to be alive, ain't it."

Pa walked over to Forrest. "What's going on here?" he asked.

"Well, I'll let Pastor Wilson feel ya in on that," he replied.

The preacher walked up and shook Pa's hand.

"You know, Zeb," he began. "We think mighty highly of the Cobb family. They're a fine couple and

133

they've been a real blessing to our church."

Pa stood there with a puzzled look on his face.

"Yet, when they came down with a true affliction, what did we do but listen to Dr. Kendree. We didn't go to visitin' like we should have or bestow a little comfort like we could have. Sure, there was a lot of bended knees askin' the Lord's mercy, but not much in the way of lending a shoulder or holding a hand."

"I don't see what that has to do with y'all being in my yard," interrupted Pa.

"Well, Zeb," the preacher said, "your man here, Brother Diver."

"Hold on there," Pa bristled. "He ain't my man. He's my friend."

"Sorry, Zeb. No offence intended," Wilson uttered. He cleared his throat.

"Hear him out, Pa," Forrest said, coming over and laying a hand on Pa's shoulder.

The preacher nodded at Forest, then continued.

"Anyway, when we heard what Brother Diver did for the Cobbs, why it was just what any good Christian should have done. I'm ashamed to say it, but it was way more than their own congregation did. So, we were looking for a way to thank the good man. You know, show him how much we appreciated him."

He looked at Diver and grinned.

"But he wouldn't have none of it. Said he hadn't passed along half of what you did for him. He told us how you shot that killer bear that near killed him, and then dove into a freezing pool of water to keep him from drowning. Said how it cost you losing the brute and the reward money too. Then he told us how you nursed him, and fed him, and drug him plumb across the mountains on an improvised travois. According to Brother Diver, there ain't another man in these hills could have done it, and I believe him. Saved his life is what you did."

Pa said, "I still don't know what this has to do with you being in my yard."

Pastor Wilson smiled, "Yes, sir, I guess you don't."

He smiled at the crowd that had gathered round.

"Well, Mr. Banion," he said, "since Bother Diver here won't take accolades for what he done, seeing how you're the real hero and all, it put us in a fix. How do you thank someone who won't accept it?

"Then, when we heard he was building a barn on

your property, we figured we would kill two birds with one stone, so to speak. So, to thank you both, we're here for a good old barn raisin'."

Pa and Diver both looked stunned.

"And you can't refuse it," Wilson added, "cause we done used that forty-dollar reward money to buy the materials. In fact, there's twelve dollars, and eighty-three cents left over."

He handed the money to Pa.

With that, the congregated men gave a cheer and began unloading timbers, planks, and shake shingles from their wagons. More men hefted tools, kegs of nails, and a few hundred feet of heavy rope, to be taken across the bridge to the building site.

Diver began laying out plans with the more knowledgeable carpenters, revising his original ideas to accommodate a much larger structure than he'd pictured. He also pointed out his staked area for the fence row which a few men decided to extent by about double.

While all this was going on, Pa pulled the preacher to the side. He handed him back the twelve dollars and eighty-three cents.

"Give this to the Cobbs," he said. "The way I hear it, they could use it. Just say it's from friends."

"That's very thoughtful of you, Brother Banion. I'm sure it will be a blessing."

Pa was a bit taken aback by the 'Brother' part of Wilson's statement. He didn't quite know what to think.

"One more thing," said the preacher. "My daughter, Mary, wanted to come along. She's sitting there in the wagon. You think your wife might like some company?"

"I'm sure she would," said Pa.

"Billy!" he hollered. "Take young Mary there in and introduce her to your Ma."

"Yes, sir, Pa," I said. He had no idea just how pleased I was to do just that.

As the racket intensified behind me--men shouting and laughing while balancing oversized framing timbers in deep pits ripped from the stone-hard ground, I tried to get Mary's attention. For some reason, I couldn't seem to find my voice. Meaning to bellow out like the townsmen at work, I only managed a gurgled murmur. Horrified, I swallowed a knot in my throat and prepared to try again. Luckily, Mary's head was bowed, and she hadn't noticed. Or had she? I saw her peep outta the corner of her eye like I'd seen her do before. I don't know why, but my belly flip-flopped and my knees 'bout turned to jelly.

When she realized I'd seen her looking, she raised her head and smiled at me.

"Oh Billy, was you talking to me?" she asked.

"You . . ." I stuttered, "M..M..Ma."

I knew I was making a fool of myself, but she just sat there like she hadn't noticed.

"I'm supposed to take you to Ma," I blurted out.

"Oh? Why thank you Billy," she said, reaching out a hand for me to help her down from the buggy.

I reached up, my heart pounding. Then, right before our hands touched, I pulled back and said, "Grab that handbrake there and climb down the wheel, I won't let ya fall."

Having no idea of how to help a young lady down from a wagon, my mind whirled. Do you lay a hand on their back? Hold their elbow? Surely, you don't touch their waist. My mouth was dry. The hairs on the back of my neck tingled. Was Ma watching from the house?

138

I turned to see.

"Eek!" I heard.

Spinning back around, I saw Mary sprawled out on the ground, staring up at me with shocked eyes. She must have fallen backward off a spoke thinkin' I'd be there to catch her.

I profusely apologized as I helped her up.

She was uncommonly quiet as she brushed off her backside on the way to the house.

A door creaked. A pig squealed. I looked up to see Ma standing on the stoop holding a squirming piglet in her arms. Her face was composed but I saw a mischievous look in her eye. I had no doubt she'd seen the whole thing. My already blazing face amped up by about fifty degrees.

"Ma, this is Mary Wilson," I stammered.

Ma had put three of the piglets into a wooden box with several old rags on the bottom and was feeding the fourth one by dribbling goat's milk into its smacking maw with a hollow reed.

See smiled and said, "Hello, Mary."

Mary saw the squirming, hungry piglets.

"Oh, they're so cute," she said, rushing into the

kitchen and kneeling down next to the box to pet them. Ma handed her the reed and showed her how to dip it in a bowl of milk while holding a finger over one end until she was ready to release it into a piglet's mouth.

"That's so clever," said Mary. She laughed as one pig sneezed milk all over her brother.

"Well, I better be seeing what I've got to feed all these men." Ma said. "Come lunch time they're gonna be awfully hungry."

"Oh, I was supposed to tell you," Mary said. "Sarah May and some of the other wives will be here in a bit to help out. They said they'll all bring along something and it will be potluck."

"That's wonderful," said Ma. "But, I'm gonna get started. Can you handle feeding the piglets okay, Mary, dear?"

"I'll be fine, Mrs. Banion," she replied. Then a bit softer, "I'm sure Billy could help me. Billy, will you help me?"

Ma heard a sound in Mary's voice that's unmistakable to a woman. She looked at me and noticed my slack-jawed stare as I nodded my head.

140

You may think you've received a reprieve, but you'd be best off runnin' for the hills, son, she thought. *You've done been snared and don't even know it.*

She cracked a smile as she turned away.

By late evening, a new double-crib barn sat on the raised bank of the creek. Each crib was sixteen feet square with a twelve-foot breezeway in between. Everything was under one shake-shingle roof.

The front crib, with a south facing doorway, had a dirt floor for the farm critters and a loft above already half filled with clover hay. Attached to the front crib was a post and rail fence that encompassed a half-acre of cleared land which gave easy access to a sloped bank of the creek.

The rear crib, with a plank floor and a door facing into the breezeway, was perfect for a toolshed and workshop. Above, up a ten-foot ladder, was a spacious sleeping loft that would soon have a Ben Franklin wood burner of its own.

Both the workshop and upper loft had spaces for shuttered windows front and back facing the creek and mountains respectively. The whole thing was built of timber framing and vertical plank siding.

The sleeping loft and a Ben Franklin stove had been Ma and Pa's idea. A gift to Diver. They figured he'd be happy to be outta Ma's kitchen. Of course, it wouldn't exactly offend Ma either.

When the evening meal was done everyone gathered round a bonfire in the field joking and laughing about the mishaps they'd encountered while building the barn. And how Pastor Wilson 'bout called down "fire and brimstone" when he hit his thumb with a hammer.

Of course, Pa and Diver had to once again retell their adventures, but so as not to kill the mood, they exaggerated the bear into a twenty-foot beast with six legs and elephant tusks. Then Diver told how he rode Pa across the streams, "guiding him the whole way by pulling on his ears".

It was about as pleasant an evening as I can recall on the homestead. Course for me, the most pleasant part was just sitting there with Mary by my side.

Finally, it was time to call it a night. Everyone loaded into their wagons and shouted out "Farewell!" and "Be safe!"

Right before Pastor Wilson flicked his horse's reins to start on the long trek home, Mary looked down at me and smiled.

"See you in school Monday, Billy," she said and winked.

I'd never looked so forward to school in my life.

After everyone was gone, Ma, Pa, and Diver sat in the kitchen for a while drinking coffee and talking about the barn, the community, and what Ma was gonna do with all them leftovers. They told Diver that'd see if Delma could have a Ben Franklin delivered in the next week or so.

I didn't join in on the family chat. I think I'd been tensed up all day without even knowing it. When it wore off, I was plumb tired. After taking a trip out back, I climbed up to my sleeping loft and in no time at all was dead to the world. That night I dreamed of Mary and butterflies.

ELEVEN

Tight Fit

SUNDAY AFTER CHURCH, Mr. Grear had Ben Cobb deliver Tilly, the Jersey cow. It was a pretty good walk so naturally Ma insisted on feeding him lunch. She then told him to stick around a while. Said Forrest was comin' to drop off another load of hay and he'd be happy to give Ben a ride back to the Cobb place. Ben didn't seem to take offense to the suggestion and even did a fair job of helpin' Ma get rid of some of them leftovers.

By Monday morning I'd developed a mighty big reservation 'bout goin' to school after all. As much as I'd enjoyed gettin' to know Mary better at the barn raisin', I just didn't know what to expect in a public situation. Would she want to sit around makin' googly eyes, as Second Chance had put it, embarrassing me in front of the whole class? Or would she play the "Ice Queen" and ignore me?

I wasn't at all sure which would be worse.

As it turned out, I needn't have fret about it. We just kinda fell back into our old routines, she with the girls, and me with the boys. As days passed, we did make eye contact now and then ... even exchanged a few polite words. But somehow, we both seemed to be hesitant about what to do next.

Then, nearly before I realized it, spring rolled 'round, school let out, and we went our separate ways. Sure, I still saw her at church on Sunday mornin's, but somehow with her Pa standin' there, lookin' down from the pulpit, it just didn't feel the same.

Diver, in the meantime had built a pretty fair pigsty behind the barn for the pigs. At nearly four months old and fifty pounds each, you couldn't rightly call them piglets anymore. The rough-plank shelter was surrounded by a twenty-foot square, post and rail fence with a stone foundation to keep em from rootin' out, or coyotes from diggin' in. About half the pen was shaded by thick hews while the lower end had a good size wallow far enough from the creek to keep em from taintin' the water.

Diver claimed a passel of hogs could poison a freshwater stream so bad it wouldn't be safe for man or beast to drink out of. As a matter of fact, there'd been cattle farmers who lost a good portion of their stock to hog tainted water.

One morning as I was sloppin' the pigs with breakfast leftovers, I heard a male eastern towhee bird call out, 'drink-your-tea', followed by the trills of a warbler. Spinning 'round, I threw my head back and was about to release my best 'bobwhite' whistle when, to my surprise, I heard the quail let loose right behind me. Looking over my shoulder I saw Pa standing there with a mischievous grin on his face.

"Sounds like Henry's waitin' on ya," he said. "Rinse out that slop bucket for your ma before you go traipsing off." He stood lookin' off in the distance. "And ask after Henry's ma for me."

I had no idea Pa knew me and Henry's 'secret' bird calls, but it weren't all that big a surprise. Seemed like he knew just about everything that happened in them mountains.

I also didn't know what connection he had with

146

Henry Rainwater. Far as I could tell, other than his own kin, he wouldn't have given a wormy acorn for any kid in the Cove. But he did seem to think somethin' highly of Henry.

"Sure, Pa," I said. I then hurried down to the creek and rinsed out the slop bucket before placing it near the back door where Ma kept it.

"Got the pigs slopped Ma," I called through the open kitchen doorway. "Goin' with Henry. See ya later."

With that, I headed for the woods. I didn't even hear Ma call back to be careful and not miss supper.

Henry was waiting at our usual meeting spot on top of a large flat-top boulder, across the creek from Pa's tannin' shed.

"Looks like y'all been busy," Henry said as I climbed up next to him. "Got ya a new barn and a fenced pasture and a bridge. I see a cow and a goat and what's that in the corral by them evergreens?"

"Them's pigs," I said. I then proceeded to tell Henry all about Pa's bear hunt, and savin' Diver, and Diver's savin' old man Cobb, and the barn raisin', and the cow, and the goat, and the pigs. Then almost as an afterthought, I said, "And I got something to show ya."

"What's that?" Henry asked.

"Just follow me," I replied as I scooted over to the edge of the boulder and jumped off.

With a quick tumble I was on my feet racing through the wooded landscape along the base of a steep hillside.

In no time, Henry was right on my heels.

"Where we goin'?" he shouted.

"Just come on," I huffed back. "You'll see soon enough."

In less than five minutes I tumbled to the ground.

Henry, not even breathing hard, flopped down beside me.

"We're here," I said, trying to catch my breath.

Henry looked around seeing nothing but trees, rhododendrons, and a steep hillside.

"We're where?" he asked. "I don't see nothin' special."

I grinned a big ol' possum-in-a-persimmon-tree grin.

"You gotta know the backwoods to see what

148

others don't see. Someday I'll teach ya all about it."

Henry pulled up a handful of plantain and threw it at me. "Right, Cove boy," he said. "That'd be like a field mouse teachin' a blue jay to fly."

Laughing, I rolled over and swept back some dangling rhododendrons revealing the entrance to the cave me and Diver had found.

"Don't underestimate us field mice," I said.

"Whoa," said Henry as he stood up and came over to examine the cave entrance. "Have ya been inside?"

"Yeah," I said. "Me and Diver went in when we first found it. At least, we went into the only room we saw. We were gonna come back with torches to check it out better, but never got around to it."

Henry slid behind the plant life and disappeared inside. I quickly followed.

Standing there looking around in the dim light from the crack in the ceiling, Henry said, "We need to start a fire and check this place out."

"Yeah? I thought you'd see it that way," I said.

Nothing thrilled Henry like a new adventure.

Leaving the cave, I gathered a bunch of twigs and dry sticks while Henry searched a nearby birch grove for "birch tinder fungus". The black fungus that grows on white birch trees, when ground to a powder, makes a fine fire starter.

Returning with a leafy pouch in his hands, he met me back at the cave and proceeded to crush the contents with a flat rock. In no time at all he had a small, pulverized pile of tinder fungus which he poured on the stone floor beneath the twigs. He then used the flint and steel he always carried in a small leather bag strung around his neck to spark a flame to life. A few soft blows, some well-placed twigs, and he soon had a blazing campfire centered on the cavern floor.

I've often thought ol' Henry could start a fire at the bottom of an Artesian well if he put his mind to it.

As we sat around talking, we placed the ends of a few three-foot-long cedar sticks into the flame. They were about as thick as our wrists, and when lit, gave off sufficient enough torchlight to examine the cave with.

On the natural shelf at the back of the room, and scattered here and there on the floor, were bits and pieces of dried bones from a variety of small animals.

Leaves and twigs had fallen in through the crack above and while scraping them aside we soon learned to be careful not to step in dried animal scat. Seemed the occasional fox or racoon made its home there. All in all, your basic single chamber cave.

Then Henry called, "Hey Billy, come and take a look at this."

I rushed over. He had his torch extended into a crevice at the end of the rock shelf.

"How big is it?" I asked.

"Plenty big to crawl inside," he said. "But I can't see how deep it is."

With that, (did I mention Henry loved adventure?) he began squirming his way inside. I watched him disappear.

"Be careful Henry," I shouted.

After hearing him shimmy around in the passage for a while, I laid on the floor and stretched my torch into the space to see what was going on. I could just make out the soles of his moccasin covered feet round a bend in the narrow crawl.

"Henry!" I shouted.

"I'm okay," he called back. "But the passage got a

lot tighter after the bend. I'm on my side pulling with my fingers and pushing with my toes. I don't think I can back up."

I listened to several grunts as I watched the dim flickering of his dwindling torchlight. Then a muffled voice reached my ears.

"I see somewhere to turn around," he gasped. "It's a crack in the wall. If I can get my feet and legs into it, I think I can flip over."

Just then the dim light I was watching went out.

"Billy!" I heard him cry. "My torch went out! It's black as pitch in here! I can barely make out your light. Whatever you do, don't let it die."

I laid my torch on the tunnel floor and scrambled back to the fire for another one. When I returned with the fresh light, I called out, "Are you okay?"

At first, there was nothing but the pounding of my own heart in my ears. I'll tell ya, I was gettin' worried. If he was stuck, anyone tryin' to crawl in to help him was likely to get stuck too. And there was no way of digging him out through a solid stone mountain. I didn't know what to do. Should I go fetch Pa? Should I stay to keep the torch lit?

Then, after what seemed like an eternity, I heard an excited voice.

"I got turned around!" he called. "I'm comin' out."

A few minutes later I saw Henry's dirt-streaked face appear from around the bend. Then his body. I moved the torches out of the way, and he came scrambling from the crevice into the main chamber.

"You 'bout scared the tar outta me," I said.

"Didn't do myself a whole lotta good either," he grinned. "After that bend, the passage got so narrow I had to turn on my side. It was plenty tall, but not wide enough to lay flat. I was stretched out straight and could only use my fingertips and toes to pull and push myself along.

"At first, I tried to back up, but with the way I was layin', I couldn't get my legs around the bend. I'm tellin' ya, that got my heart to beatin'. Anyway, I had no choice but to go forward. I'd push the torch a few inches, then squeezed up to it, then do it all over again. I'll admit, I was getting a tad nervous. Then, somethin' Pa used to say came to me.

"'Ain't nothin' to be scared of unless ya give up.'

"Then I saw a crack in the wall about five feet in

153

front of me. It wasn't much, but I figured if I could jam my legs into it, I might be able to sit up, flop over, and crawl back out."

He wiped a sheen of sweat off his forehead.

"The passage was narrow, but it was tall enough to sit up and turn over in. Anyway, I wiggled ahead and almost got to the crack when I noticed a dark area maybe another ten feet in front of me. I think it was another room. But then, wouldn't you know it, my torch went out. You ain't never seen that kinda darkness. I'm talkin' absolute blackness."

As he talked my pulse pounded so hard you'd o' thought I was the one that'd been stuck.

"I'm man enough to admit it," he continued. "I wasn't just nervous anymore. No matter what Pa said, I was downright scared. But what are you gonna do? Panicking will kill ya.

"I laid there with my eyes closed for a bit to try and calm down. Then I steeled myself and figured I had no choice but to continue by feel. I mean, there's no way anyone else could have gotten me outta there. I had to do it on my own.

"When I finally felt the crack, I crawled a little

way past it, pressed up against the opposite wall, pulled my knees and feet in tight, and jammed them in. Having accomplished that, I sat up, laid over, and like to of ripped my shins off scrambling outta there."

He laughed.

"For a moment there, I didn't think I was gonna make it. But man, oh man, it sure does make fresh air taste mighty sweet."

I figured, like any sane person would, that our cave exploring was over. I was wrong.

"We gotta make better torches," Henry said.

"Better torches?" I sputtered.

We sat there on the shelf for quite a spell tellin' tales, laughin', and havin' a good ol' time. I told Henry about Tyrone and his buds on the bridge and how I was fixin' to hurt 'em bad before Diver showed up.

Henry laughed and allowed how they surely did have a close call.

Then Henry told me about believin' he saw the shapeshifter change from a bear into a wolf during a snowstorm last December. He said his Ma saw it too but won't admit it.

I didn't mention Mary or our day together. I

figured that was between me and her.

As the day grew long, I invited Henry home for supper. Told him Ma would be right proud to have him. He said he appreciated it, but he'd told his Ma he wouldn't be late. Black Gum Shoal was better than an hour from our place as Henry went at a steady run. Three or four times as far by pack mule or wagon.

How he made that run both ways in a single day was beyond me, but when I asked him about it, he said, "A Cove dweller would never understand."

I told him we didn't live in the Cove, but he just laughed and said, "And a hawk don't live in the sky."

I wasn't sure how to answer that. Technically, they don't.

Before Henry left, we agreed our next adventure to the cave would be with pine knot torches at the least, and tallow candles if possible.

"We could spend the night," Henry suggested.

I wasn't too thrilled about that idea, but I didn't want him to think I was scared.

"Maybe after the ramp picnic," I said.

The ramp picnic was a community affair that took place each spring on any one of several balds around the Cove. Whole families would gather to dig ramps, or wild leeks as some folks called em, and make a weekend of it. The garlicky plants were quite abundant in spring, above three thousand feet and were a staple in most Cove kitchens.

"Okay," said Henry, jumping on my comment. "The ramp picnic is next weekend. Let's say the following Monday. It'll be an adventure."

I felt my stomach churn. Another adventure! But what could I say? At least I knew we wouldn't be messing with that crawl. What could go wrong?

"I'll have Ma make us some snacks," I said.

Before Henry headed out, I remembered to ask after his mother for Pa. He said she claimed to be doing good, but sometimes he wondered. Neither of us could figure why they lived on Black Gum Shoal all alone. Henry had once asked, but his mother wouldn't say. All he knew was that occasionally someone left meat hanging in a tree near their cabin. Henry thought it might be the old shaman, Two Hand, but why would a shapeshifter feed a widow and her son?

I guess some things just aren't for twelve-year-olds to know.

As it was gettin' late in the day, Henry said his goodbyes and headed into the hills. I watched him out of sight, then turned for home myself. I knew by the time I got there it would be time to milk Ma's goat along with Tilly, the cow. If I'd been late Diver would have done it, but I'd promised Pa I'd do more chores around the place. I kinda liked the way he looked at me when I said that. Like I was carrying my own weight and all.

Yeah, I figured Ma had herself three good men 'round the place watchin' over her. Never even occurred to me, in reality, she was the one doin' most the carin'.

TWELVE

God's Jewel

W HILE ME AND HENRY were testing fate in the cave, Diver had been out traipsing through the woods as was his habit when not busy around the homestead. As of late he'd began carryin' a long-handled shovel, either over his shoulder or blade end up like a heavy-headed walking stick. We thought nothing of it, seein's how he often brought home interesting or unusual plants and roots to study or use around the farm.

The night of the cave adventure, havin' my chores done and my face and hands washed, I bellied-up to the kitchen table and impatiently sat waitin' for Diver to say grace. It's downright amazin' how a gut-wrenching scare can peak a growing boy's appetite.

Ma, as always, the last person off her feet, settled

tight jawed and head bowed into her chair. She uttered not a peep, but I got the feeling somethin' wasn't setting right with her. Lookin' 'round I saw the culprit right off. It was Diver.

Diver, under most conditions well-mannered and well-kept, was uncommonly disheveled. He had beggar's lice clinging to one soiled sleeve, traces of dried oak leaves scattered in his hair, and a V-shaped piece of tattered cloth dangling from his torn shirt collar.

Now don't get me wrong, we certainly didn't dress up for dinner, but slovenliness wasn't something Ma appreciated. If it hadn't been that it was Diver, I don't think it would have gone without mention that day. And I whole heartedly doubted it would again.

When it came to eatin' 'round our place, we stood on few formalities at all. If you wanted something, you plopped it on your plate and reached for the next item. I learned early on you don't contemplate too long about it either. Pa had a mighty fast fork.

Diver scooped out a mess of black-eyed peas and grabbed a large chunk of hot cornbread. As he cut it open and began slathering on home-churned butter he said, "Went up on the north ridge today."

"That right?" Pa said as he stabbed a slab of elk roast. "What ya doing up that away?"

"Oh, just moseying around," Diver replied as he gave Ma a sideways glance. "Happened to come on a honey tree near that south facing lookout."

Ma perked up right off. "Honey?" she said placing her fork on her plate. She looked from Diver to Pa. "I'd sure admire me a mess o' fresh honey."

Pa nodded, "Yeah, reckon that'd go right nice with some cornbread or a hot cup o' coffee." He looked at Diver, "Bout when ya figure it'll be ready to harvest?"

Me and Ma were both on pins and needles waitin' for Diver's answer.

He took a moment to think it over. "You know, regularly, I'd say early fall at the soonest, but we had us a pretty mild winter. I reckon them bees collected late and didn't hafta go through all their reserves, so I'm thinkin' late July or early August oughta do it."

Ma did some quick cipherin'. "That'd be about five or six weeks," she said.

"Sounds about right," Pa said. "How much ya reckon we'll get out of it?" he asked Diver.

"Well, from what I could see, it's a pretty fair hive. I'd say sixty to eighty pounds would be reasonable."

"Sixty to eighty pounds!" Ma gasped. Her eyes lit up like a polecat findin' the hen house door open.

"On top of that," continued Diver. "If we take a bit of care, I reckon we can catch the queen and move the whole hive back here."

Ma actually clapped her hands and said, "Praise the Lord!"

Pa nearly spewed a mouth full of coffee. "I ain't seen you so excited since Forrest brought ya them scrawny piglets to play nursemaid too."

"Yeah?" Ma retorted. "Well, when you go to eatin' them scrawny piglets cured in fresh wild honey and slow smoked over a bed of hickory coals, you'll be as happy as a pup in a gut pile."

Pa laughed. "You got me there," he said. "And Kathryn, there ain't a body in this whole range can do what you can to a good ol' pile o' guts."

"Oh, hooey!" Ma said as she threw a dish rag at him. "Such talk comin' from a man what spends half his life eaten wormy acorns and frost-bitten huckleberries in some dank and dark, backwoods

162

canyon. May as well be praise from an undersized catfish that was pitch back in the pond."

After supper, Diver offered to take the scraps too the pigs and asked Pa to accompany him.

I had no idea what Diver was up to, but it dawned on me that I was one chore down. Thank you Diver.

As they strolled out the door and down to the bridge, Diver said, "I ran into Clarence Tudwell the other day."

"Too bad for you," said Pa.

Diver ignored the sarcasm in Pa's voice and continued. "Seems he's got a mule team and wagon he's looking to part with."

Pa watched as Diver poured the slop bucket into the feeding trough causing a fray to break out as four squealing pigs attacked the swill.

"Yeah, he's got a good-lookin' team," Pa allowed bein' a fast admirer of the stout beasts. "What of it?"

"Well, I was thinking it might be nice to have a way to get around a little better," said Diver. "You know, like a way for Kate to visit with Forrest's family or go to church, or whatnot."

Pa stiffened.

"Kathryn ain't never complained to me about not gettin' around," Pa said.

Diver thumped the bucket on a fence post a couple times to knock loose the last clingin' scraps.

"I know she ain't," he said. "You got a good woman there. Complainin' ain't in her nature." He flicked a piece of apple rind off his finger. "But I got another reason for thinkin' we could use a good mule team."

"That right? What you got in mind?" Pa asked as they headed toward the creek to rinse out the bucket.

"You may have noticed I been carryin' a shovel 'round lately," said Diver.

Pa nodded, "Hafta be blind not to."

"There's a reason for that," said Diver. He dipped the bucket in the stream, swirled it around, and poured it out. "I found some land on your property that I believe would raise a fine crop of corn. The only problem is we'd hafta clear it of brush. That's where the mules come in."

Pa looked at him like he'd claimed he was Noah.

"You been feeling that fever comin' back lately?" Pa stammered. "You're talking outta your head. Ain't

164

no land of mine could grow broom corn, much less flint or sweet."

"By all regular reasonin' you'd be correct," said Diver as they headed back toward the house. "But I got something to show ya tomorrow. Problem is, I don't know if we can manage it without a mule."

"Well then, we're outta luck," said Pa taking the bucket from Diver and putting it in its place by the back door. "Cause, Clarence Tudwell wouldn't sell me a mule team and wagon even if I had the money to buy it... which I ain't!"

"Now, that may not be exactly accurate," said Diver. "The way I hear it, the trouble between you and Clarence began when he fenced his south pasture for some beef cattle he bought off Orwell Beckett and they found their way onto your property."

"It's a might more than that," said Pa, "but we'll say that's right. He kept his dairy cows on his own land where they belonged, but he let loose them beef cattle down there where they could cross the creek and get free grazin' off o' my land. Said it was unintentional, but what good does that do me?"

"Clarence tells me he offered to pay you in milk

for the grass his cattle ate."

"And then I'm supposed to run around selling his milk?" said Pa. "No thanks. I told him any cows I caught on my property would wind up in my smokehouse."

"Well, I think I may have a solution," said Diver. "Clarence says, if you agree to let him use your lower pasture along the creek, he'll fence it off so his cows can't stray, trade you the mule team and wagon for the first year's rent and give you one cow to butcher for each year's rent thereafter. That's for as long as the contract lasts."

Pa had to admit it was a fair deal. Then, Two Hand and the Rainwaters came to mind. If he agreed to a bargain, maybe he could help them out to boot.

"Tell him to make it two cows and I'll throw in one whitetail and twenty pounds of honey along with the land."

"I'll make the offer," said Diver.

When I came down to breakfast next mornin', Ma plucked a few strands of straw from my tousled hair then said how she'd seen Diver walkin' down the Cove trail when she went out to collect the eggs. Said she had no idea where he might be a headin' off to but just chalked it up to Diver bein' Diver.

I allowed how he sure could be a mystery sometimes. I then hurried out back before headin' over to milk Tilly and the goat. Finishin' up, I poured the cow's milk into a clean milk can for coolin' in the springhouse and slopped the pigs with the goat's milk. One thing I can tell ya sure, we had us some mighty happy pigs. Course, it's true, they didn't know what was comin' in the fall. Such is life on a farm.

By the time I'd stored away Tilly's offering's and lugged a cold can to the cabin, Ma had a pot of coffee heatin' by the fire. She looked up and smiled as she began slicing a slab of bacon taken from a wild hog Pa had shot off Orwell's wheat field the week before. I placed the sweet milk next to the eggs and butter and eyed a hot loaf of cooling sourdough bread straight out of the Dutch oven. My mouth watered. My fingers inched toward a kitchen knife.

"Don't even think about it," Ma said without even looking.

I deflated in defeat and sat on a kitchen chair.

Not two minutes later, Pa, having washed up in

167

the tin tub we kept out back, came in and poured himself his first cup of morning coffee. He reached over to pinch a chunk of bread.

Wop!

Pa snatched back his hand as the wooden spoon made contact.

"What?" he burst, startled.

"Where do ya think Diver was off to so early this mornin'," Ma asked as if nothing had happened.

Pa stood shaking his hand. "I don't know," he said. "Last he told me; he had somethin' to show me this mornin'."

He looked at me with questioning eyes as he rubbed his knuckles.

I turned my head and tried not to laugh.

"Well, he was hoofin' it down the trail when I went out for eggs," Ma said.

"When it comes to Diver, a person would be hard pressed to know what he's up to," Pa stated.

As he turned his back to find his seat, Ma glanced at me and winked with a sly grin on her face. I was plumb tickled that I wasn't the only one who needed to know his place in her kitchen.

168

When we'd finished our breakfast and sat talking as Pa poured himself a third cup of coffee, we heard a jangling sound out front along with the clip-clop of iron shod hooves.

"What's that?" Ma uttered. "You ain't expecting Forrest this mornin', are ya?"

"Not that I'm aware of," said Pa.

We all got up and went to the front door.

"I'll be!" gasped Ma as she took hold of Pa's arm. "Now, Zeb, don't get yourself all fired up. Let's see what's goin' on."

It was a sight I never thought I'd live to see. Diver and Mr. Tudwell were standing right there in Pa's front yard. Behind them was a buckboard and mule team.

"How do, Zeb?" Mr. Tudwell said as he walked over and held out his hand.

I noticed Pa flinch when Ma pinched him in the ribs.

"Tudwell?" Pa said as he took the proffered shake.

Well, you coulda knocked me over with a Banty hen feather. I don't reckon there'd ever been more contrary neighbors in the whole of Tennessee, and

169

here they were, shakin' hands.

"Diver told me what all you did for us cattle farmers, takin' on that bear the way you done," Clarence said. "And how you figured a way we could profit from being neighbors rather than fightin' all the time. Then he mentioned how you said you'd throw in twenty pounds of honey just to sweeten the pot, so to speak."

He pulled his hat off his head and wiped the sweat from his hair with a calico bandana.

"Well, Zeb, I'm man enough to admit I've been wrong about you all along."

Then, turning to his mules, he said, "This here big boy, I call Mac. He's a might bit stubborn now and again, but I ain't never seen a harder worker."

Pa admired the large beast of burden. He had a coat as black as midnight and looked as solid as the stones at chimney rock.

"And this young lady," Clarence continued, "is Joleen. She's just about the sweetest thing you ever laid eyes on. Tell ya the truth," he said as he scratched behind her long ears, "it ain't gonna feel right not hearin' her cockamamie bray in the mornin's."

170

He then led Pa to the wagon.

"And, by the way, if you look in here, you'll find I threw in all the tack you'll be needin'. If I missed anythin', you just let me know."

Pa stood speechless for a moment, till Diver cleared his throat breaking the silence.

Like a clap of thunder, it occurred to Pa what had happened. Diver had set them both up. Made em both feel grateful for the generosity of the other.

He smiled and said, "Well, Clarence, I reckon it's only right that neighbors look out for one another. Why don't you come on in and have a cup of coffee?"

Pa figured he and Diver was gonna have a sit-down about this later.

As the new friends headed into the cabin, side by side with a grinning Diver right behind, me and Ma stood in the front yard too stunned to move.

"Never did I expect to see those two shake hands and sit down to coffee together," Ma whispered in my ear.

I nodded in agreement and looked back at the mule team and wagon. That big old woman hatin' rooster of Ma's had already claimed himself a roost on

171

the buckboard's seat.

"Hard to know what to expect since Diver showed up," I uttered.

Ma laughed and laid her hand on my shoulder. "You got that right son," she said. "God sent us a jewel when he dropped that man over them falls."

THIRTEEN

Mountain Meadow

CLARENCE TURNED DOWN Pa's offer for a ride home. Said he'd prefer to walk the lower pasture to get an idea of how much fencing he was gonna be needing. Figured this was his chance to finally get a leg up on Mr. Grear for a change.

Now, don't get me wrong, I have no doubt the two cattlemen respected each other just fine. It's just that since Mr. Tudwell had decided to diversify by adding a few beef cows to his operations, Mr. Grear had felt his domain was being imposed upon. As you may imagine, he wasn't all that happy about the situation. Not a word was spoken, but it wasn't hard to see the competitive angst that was building between the two. I just hoped that Pa wouldn't be dragged into it. Not that he'd have cared, one way or the other.

"So, how much land you reckon you got down there?" Clarence asked. "Forty, fifty acres?"

"Thereabouts," said Pa. "It'll take a heap of fencin'."

"Me and the boys'll see to it," Clarence promised.

He then shook Pa's hand one last time and headed down the hill.

I can tell ya true, that was one happy man.

"I'll park the wagon by the barn and turn the mules out to pasture," Diver said as he started towards the team.

"Hold on a minute," said Pa.

Diver stopped and turned to Pa who was just standing there holding onto his suspender's straps.

"I just wanted you to know that *I know* what you pulled there," he said.

"Can't imagine what you're talkin' about," said Diver; sincerity written all over his face.

Pa tried to keep a straight face. "I'm sure you can't," he said. "Now, what's this about showing me something that just can't be done without mules."

After parkin' the wagon and releasing the mules in the pasture with Tilly and the goat, (We never did

174

name that goat, though I don't know why) Diver pointed out a ridge on the back side of Pa's property.

"What I got to show ya is the other side of that ridge yonder," he said.

"Okay," said Pa as they stared into the distance. "But I already know what's back there. A mess o' buckbrush with a bare-backed ridge beyond it."

"That's what I wanna talk to ya about," said Diver. "Let's go take a look. Trust me — you'll be pleased you did."

Pa shook his head and laid his big hand on Diver's shoulder. "I seen a passel o' buckbrush in my day," he said, "but if you think yorn is somethin' special, let's go take a gander."

Diver chuckled. "Plumb proud ya'd put yerself out this away, just on my askin'," he said.

Pa grinned and puffed out his chest. "Just don't make a habit of it," he teased. "Takes a mighty big toll on a man to run such an empire as I got here. Ain't got time for pleasure or shenanigans."

"Ain't it the truth," Diver snickered. "Ain't it the truth. Why, I've laid awake at night just marvelin' at the magnitude of responsibility you tote on your shoulders every day."

Both men laughed like teenage school chums.

About ten minutes later they were pushing through an inclining meadow overgrown in thickets, beggar's lice, and wait-a-minute bushes. The upper end of the expanse gave way to a hardwood forest while the left side was bordered by a towering slope of bare rock. No-see-ems drifted by in great swarms clouding the air about their eyes and ears.

Diver stopped near a mound of dirt shadowing a three-foot hole.

"Wanna tell me what we're looking at?" Pa asked.

Diver looked up and said, "We're looking at a hole in the ground. The question is, what are we *not* looking at?"

Pa took his hat off and leaned over the hole. He brushed some pesky insects off his right cheek, then flagged the air in front of his eyes to get a better look. In the darkened recesses he could make out nothing more than shovel-scraped dirt walls, mangled creepers, and strands of plant roots. Not seeing any anomalies, he stepped back and shrugged.

"I don't know," he said. "How 'bout you tell me."

"Rocks!" said Diver, as if pointing out an obvious truth. "We're not looking at rocks."

Pa looked back in the hole.

"Well, I'll be Diver. You're right," he said. "You got yourself a rockless hole in the middle of a bunch of buckbrush and parasites."

Diver grinned. "No sir," he said. "I don't have a rockless hole. I have about forty acres of rockless holes. I been diggin' holes all over this meadow and they're all the same. Not a one less than twenty-four-inches deep, and many of em are at least twice that. And no more than a pebble or two in the bunch of em."

"So . . . what are you sayin'?" asked Pa.

"See that bare ridge?" said Diver, pointing at the barren slope. "See how much of that rock is wet? I walked that entire rise. There are six separate springs up there. You can't find twenty yards that ain't saturated. The way I figure it, at some point the weight of the whole thing became too much to bear. Maybe during them big earthquakes back in eleven and twelve. I reckon the whole thing tore loose and came sliding down to settle in this gully between these two ridges. That's a whole lot of topsoil."

He reached down to pick up a fist full of dirt and squished it between his fingers.

"I reckon if a couple of hard-workin' men with a good mule team were to clear this buckbrush and do some plantin', they'd wind up with as fine a crop of corn as anything the Cove has to offer."

"That how ya see it, is it," said Pa, scanning that big bare hillside and the buckbrush covered meadow.

"That's for a fact," said Diver.

"Ain't never been much of a farmer," Pa said, still fishin' for a downside to Diver's proposal.

"Don't know if I have or not," said Diver. "Seems to me it ain't but a bit of work, then standin' back while God rears the stalks. You ain't scared of a little work, are ya?"

"I'm thinkin' you got a problem with the way you use the word 'little'," said Pa.

Diver just grinned and shrugged.

"But it sure would be somethin', wouldn't it?" Pa uttered as he swattin' his arm. He then flicked away a bloody glob. "This old hard-rock and scrub-brush land of mine fetchin' in forty acres or so of prime corn?"

"Have them folks in the Cove done scratchin' their heads, I reckon," said Diver.

Pa nodded. "And like ya said, ain't nothing but some work."

"I walked this land over quite a spell," continued Diver. "I figure most of this buckbrush could be pulled roots and all with a good mule or two. Then there's about a half dozen or so stumps to remove. That would take a bit more doin', but I reckon we could handle it."

He pointed off into the distance.

"That little finger of woods down yonder at the bottom of the slope ain't worth messin' with," he said. "Nor the hardwoods up top. Too many boulders. But I'm thinkin' we could have the meadow cleared in no more than a month or so. Might be too late to plant this year, 'cept maybe some winter wheat, but we'd be sittin' pretty for next spring."

"Well now, let me ponder on this for a moment," said Pa. "I'm thinkin' we might could pull off a crop this year after all."

He stood there scratching his chin for a bit and

then nodded his head as if coming to a decision.

"You look around and decide how you want to go about this." he said. "I reckon you're the man in charge. I gotta make a trip to the Cove. One way or another, we may as well get at it come sun-up."

"Sounds good to me," said Diver with a hint of amusement in his eyes. It tickled him how when Pa made up his mind about somethin', he didn't let no moss grow under his feet.

With that, Pa turned toward the Cove, and Diver started plotting out the best way to clear the new cornfield.

As for me, I'd been tellin' Ma all about the cave me and Diver had found, and about how Henry and me had checked it out. Course, I didn't say nothin' about the passage, or how Henry 'bout got stuck, or anything like that. Ma loved hearin' about adventures and all, but not when they placed her family in harm's way. I'd learned from way back, it's okay to take risks in the doin', but if you ever wanna do it again, it better be safe in the tellin'.

Anyway, I told her about the narrow opening behind the rhododendrons which leads into the small, cavernous room. I then told her about the ceiling crack that makes a quite effective vent for a campfire, and how there was a shelf along the back wall that would make a great bed site well above the cold vapers wafting across the floor. Finally, once I felt I had her interest piqued, I told her what this was all leadin' up too. How, if it was alright with her and Mrs. Rainwater, me and Henry wanted to spend the night there next Monday evening after the ramp picnic.

"I don't know," said Ma, with a concerned look on her face. "How do I know if it would be safe?"

"What could happen?" I asked. "It's like a big old, secure, stone room. Why, I wouldn't be any safer right here in my own loft. Ask Diver."

There was still doubt in her eyes.

"And it's not far either," I continued. "It can't be better than a ten-minute walk from here."

"Well?" The indecision was etched across her face. "I'll talk it over with your Pa."

"Thanks Ma," I said. "He won't mind. Not if I'm with Henry. Now let's see, I reckon I'll be needin' some jerky, corn dodgers, sassafras tea, a ground cover, 'bout four tallow candles, and . . ."

"Hold on there," Ma said, laughing at my enthusiasm. "Are ya plannin' on spendin' the night or movin' in?"

I grinned. "Guess I got a bit carried away there, didn't I?"

"That's okay," she said, givin' my hair a quick roughin', the way ma's will do.

She suddenly stopped and gave me a quick once-over.

"You're 'bout due a haircut," she said.

"Aw, Ma," I groaned.

"And one more thing. You know your Pa ain't gonna be lettin' you get outta your chores."

"I know, Ma. I'll do my evenin' chores before we go, and I'll be back in time for my mornin' chores."

"What's this about chores?" Pa blurted, knowing good and well he'd caught us off guard.

We both jumped and spun around. We hadn't heard him come in.

Ma twisted her apron in her hands as she proceeded to tell him about the plans me and Henry were making, and how she wasn't sure about it, so she'd said she'd leave it up to him.

182

Of course, I couldn't leave it at that, so I jumped in sayin's how I wouldn't be missin' any chores or nothin', and I'd be with Henry.

"Diver knows where this cave is?" he asked.

"Yes sir," I said. "It was me and Diver that found it. It's in that holler the other side of the ridge, across from your tannin' shed."

He thought about that for a moment.

"I reckon you're old enough to loosen the leash on a bit," he said. "But I best not be hearin' that Diver did your chores. He's got plenty to do his own self."

"No, sir," I said. "You can count on me. And thanks Pa."

I had an urge to hug the man but thought better of it.

With that, I dashed through the door and headed out to find Diver. I'm no fool. When you get your way, you get gone before anyone can change their mind. I also wanted to let Diver know what was going on, so he'd be prepared when Ma started bombarding him with questions.

Pa cringed when the door slammed behind me.

"That boy sure knows when to make an exit," he

said.

"I hope letting them go is the right thing to do," Ma sighed. "Two young boys camping out all alone like that; it frightens me."

Pa could see the concern etched on her brow.

"Now, don't you go frettin' 'bout them boys Kathryn," he said, placing both hands on the sides of her face and tilting her head back to look up at him. "They ain't gonna be but a stone's throw away. Now, I got some business to take care of in the Cove. I figured I may as well try out that new mule team. You wanna go along? Maybe stop by Forrest's place for a bit?"

"I'd love to," cried Ma, her fears fading to some distant recess in her mind just as he'd hoped they would.

"Well, go grab your wrap and I'll hitch up the team."

As they left the homestead, Ma was lookin' about as happy as she had in a long, long time. And to tell ya the truth, Pa weren't no hangdog neither.

FOURTEEN

Ramps

THE PREVIOUS FALL, shortly after Pa left Gregory Bald in search of the killer bear, Percy and his group set up blinds near the dead cows in the meadow from which to keep a two-day vigil. During that time, they killed two bears: a healthy four-year-old sow, and a young boar. By the end of the second day, they were outta food, outta patience, and quite frankly, outta nerve. To alleviate the stress and boredom, it was agreed they would go down to the Cove to restock their supplies, get a home-cooked meal, and a good night's sleep. They would then return to kill the culprit.

As is often the case when good friends get together for particularly manly ventures, boastful banter and chest-thumping rhetoric flowed across the

185

forested mountainside alluding to the ferocious battle and personal accolades that laid ahead. Visions of triumph and fame abounded. Yet, after they split up, and each man went his own way, nasty little visions of impending peril began creeping into their psyches. First one, then another, suddenly remembered a myriad of pressing matters that urgently needed to be addressed around the house. Matters that unfortunately just couldn't wait. For the time being, the hunt would have to be called off. Maybe they could try again in a week or so.

By morning, only Percy was prepared to leave. But alas, with the insistence of his wife that he not go alone, even he bowed out.

The denizens of the wilds were left at peace to cleanse the carnage in the meadow. Bears, panthers, and wolves, followed by hogs, coons, foxes and skunks, each took their turns at the windfall. Then it was up to the true cleaning crew of the mountains to mop up: the field mice, insects, and birds.

By the time Thom Grear checked the clearing in preparation for the spring ramp picnic, nothing remained except a few scattered bones, which he gathered up and pitched off a nearby prominence.

Yet, even with the area cleared of all vestiges of last year's slaughter, few people from the Cove made the strenuous trip to the popular bald. They seemed to prefer Andrew's Bald, or Hemphill Bald, or maybe Spencer's Field.

Most Gregory Bald regulars claimed to be simply trying out more interesting and perhaps more productive locales that year.

As for me, I think they were afraid of the haints and boogers that follow death. No matter how much folks denied it, there was a mighty big fear of haints and boogers in the deep mountains. After all, it was common knowledge that if a body died before it's time, it might up and decide it ain't goin'. When that happens, you got yourself a booger. But the frightening part is, is it a good booger, or a bad booger? I reckon most folks figured it was safest to simply not wait around and see. To just stay clear of Gregory Bald for a while.

Well now, my brother Forrest took after Pa. He wasn't one to put no percentages in haints and boogers and whatnot. He and his family were fixin' to

187

spend the weekend on Gregory Bald for the ramp digging picnic just the same as they did every year. And since Pa and Diver were busy plantin' the cornfield, he stopped by to pick me and Ma up on his way through.

Most of the previous week, he and his crew had helped Pa and Diver clear that field in the mountains. How Pa had convinced Orwell to loan out not only a work crew, but an ox and three plows was nothing short of a miracle. All Forrest knew was it had something to do with twenty hogs, and a past debt involving a mammoth jack mule.

Ma had been a bit concerned about the weather. An old injury of her left wrist was telling her a spring shower was fixing to show. Forrest listened to her concerns, but assured her she'd be sharing the open-faced herder's shelter with Sarah May and the kids. Rain or not, they'd be fine. So, throwing our bedding in the wagon, we loaded up and were on our way. Forrest, Ma, and Sarah May sat on the spring seat up front while me and the kids occupied the bed.

It was a beautiful Saturday mornin' with clear skies after an early mist that lifted around breakfast

188

time. The trees and brush along the mountain trails sparkled in the sunlight with a light coating of dew on the foliage. Colorful yellow hooded warblers flickered around from leaf to leaf and stem to stem, as if showing off in front of some nearby grosbeaks. As I sat half daydreaming, I caught a flash of movement outta the corner of my eye. Turning, I saw a blue-tailed, five-lined skink, race along the sideboard. Quick as a flash, all three laughing kids scrambled across the straw-ladened wagon trying to catch it. It was no contest. The little lizard slipped between two rails and disappeared.

"What kind was it, Uncle Billy?" little Wes asked me as he eyed the space where it had scampered away.

"It was a skink," I said.

He laughed and grabbed his nose.

"What's going on back there?" Forrest asked.

"It was a lizard, Pa," Wes said, "and I most ketched it."

"And, what kinda lizard did you almost catch?" asked Forrest.

"It was a skunk lizard," said Wes, laughing, "and

189

it was fast."

Forrest laughed too, "A skunk lizard, you say. Was it black and white, with a big fluffy striped tail?"

"Don't be silly, Pa," Wes giggled, slappin' the air as if swattin' the question away. "You know lizards don't got furry tails. They's bald all over."

Sarah May and Ma were gettin' a kick outta the father/son banter. Sarah reached up and tousled Forrest's slightly receding hairline.

"Don't reckon your part skunk lizard yerself, do ya?" she teased.

Ma got so tickled she nearly fell outta the wagon.

We carried on jokin' and laughing 'bout skunk lizards and bald-headed foremen the rest of the way to the parking area below Gregory Bald.

The last mile or so to the bald was too rugged to get a wagon up, so we always packed our baggage on our horses or mules to finish the trek on foot.

"Everybody out," Forest called as he reined in the team and helped Ma and Sarah May down from the bench seat.

I noticed right off that another wagon, along with Pastor Wilson's buggy, were already parked in the little clearing with the occupants and animals gone beyond sight up the ridge trail.

"Y'all go ahead," Forrest told Sarah May and Ma. "Me and Billy will get the team loaded and be right behind ya."

It didn't take long before we were on our way, and by late morning were greeted by Pastor Wilson, Mary, and the Grears along with their three little uns.

"Anyone else comin' or are we it?" asked Mr. Grear.

"Chance and his family oughta be here soon," said Forrest. "Other than that, I don't know."

"From what I'm hearin', most the regulars decided against comin' up this year," said Pastor Wilson. "Some of those backwoods' booger stories are hard to put to rest. Sorry state for a Christian community if you ask me."

He had just finished dragging his heavy tarp over a ridge pole and was tackin' down the corners.

"Well, perhaps young Clinton will have a decent turn out for his first Sunday service," he finished.

"Amen to that," said Mr. Grear.

Young Clinton was a fellow Baptist theologian

who was working his way through the countryside filling in where he could as he learned his craft. Come fall he hoped to be in Georgia leading his own flock.

Our first order of business was to get busy putting up our own tents and sprucin' up the herder's shelter for Ma and Forrest's family. With everyone pitchin' in, it was easy work, and by the time we were done, Chance's clan had shown up, dogs and all.

A quick snack, and we started ramp diggin'.

The thing you gotta know about ramps is, though they flourish in the same location year after year, they're extremely slow growers. If ya over-dig your patch, you'll destroy the lot of it, and it may not come back. For that reason, each family had their own growths which they nourished along and took care of. Not that there weren't thousands of ramp patches all over the mountains, but with a digging season of less than a month, which didn't leave a whole lot of time to be traipsing about, it was just easier to work what was yours rather than look for new ones.

While the adults dug along the surrounding slopes, the younger kids had the whole meadow to explore in. They only had to remember one rule.

"Never go into the woods alone!"

Everyone remembered six-year-old Danny Davis. How he'd joyfully chased a spotted fawn into the forest one day around noon. That was eight years ago, and he'd not been seen since.

A search of the area had been fruitless, even though as word spread men throughout the entire Cove joined in the search. No one could understand how he'd simply vanished. It was unimaginable. Just one more page in the eerie tales and superstitions of the mountains.

Mary had been selected to watch over the kids while I helped Ma, and Second Chance assisted his family. The three of us wouldn't be able to get together until later that afternoon.

The first day of ramp digging was usually devoted to clearing back encroaching undergrowth and trying to decide how much produce could be prudently harvested from that patch, on that year. Due to the long weary trek up the mountain, our botanical aspirations traditionally ended with the heat of the day. We'd put what ramps had been taken in a cool, shaded place to help prevent wilting and head back to camp. The true harvest happened on the morning of the second day. That was so the delicate, garlicky greens, suffered little on the long trek home. Once there, some would be eaten fresh, while others were placed with their roots in water, so they'd keep for days. Still more ramps would be dried, smoked, or pickled, to last throughout the year.

While the ramp picnic was the traditional digging weekend, we did go out and get what we could in the following weeks before the leaves turned brown and wilted. It seemed everybody loved the pungent green, and it made for a great time getting together; after all, we mightn't see some folks again till the nut and berry picnic in the fall.

As mid-afternoon neared, we all climbed back up to the meadow lookin' forward to delicious food, great company, and just havin' a good time.

As soon as we could, Second Chance, Mary, and myself, snuck away where we could talk without the adults listening in. It didn't take long before the local gossip started flowing.

Second Chance told us how Forrest had talked Orwell Beckett into helpin' them expand their house now that his ma had another young'un on the way.

Mary talked about the plans her father had for holdin' a baptism in Abrams Creek come fall. She said he'd be invitin' the whole community, Methodists and Baptists alike.

When it was my turn, I told 'em about the cave me and Diver found and how me and Henry Rainwater was plannin' to spend the night there on Monday.

"What do you think, Chance? You want to come along?" I asked.

Second Chance thought about that for a minute. "Don't think Pa would let me," he said. "Him bein' busy workin' on the house an all, I'm supposed to be keepin' the kids from pesterin' Ma."

"Well, I wish *I* could come," said Mary.

I turned a bit red at that. Seemed Mary did me that way quite a lot that year.

"Mary, you know you can't come campin' with two boys," I said.

"I know," said Mary. "I just mean it ain't fair. You boys getta have all the fun."

I really didn't know what to say to that, but I was

195

saved when Pastor Wilson called for Mary to come an eat. We all jumped up and headed for the food line. The shared potluck ramp picnic was not to be missed.

After Pastor Wilson said grace, and Chance Sr. chased Blue Boy and Ricket away from the table, we all settled in and had a fine meal with lots of talking, joke tellin', and stories. Just a good ol' time. Ma astounded everyone, tellin' them about Pa and Clarence Tudwell sitting down to coffee. And Pastor Wilson shared his plans for having the big fall baptizing in Abrams Creek. Then Chance and Forrest both talked about the room additions they were adding to Chance's house.

The one thing I noticed that no one was talking about, was poor Joey Cobb. I reckon seein's how he'd passed at the far end of the very same meadow we were sitting in, not more than a mile away, that's understandable.

As conversation slowed and a beautiful orange and red sunset spread out over the distant peaks, Forrest and Chance Senior gathered up the food scraps and wrapping em in a tarp, carried them well away from camp hanging it from a high limb. That was to dissuade unwanted night visitors, even though we knew if a denizen of the forest were to come too close, Blue Boy and Ricket would sound the alarm and chase them away.

As the light faded and thousands of crickets took up their nightly serenade, Wes and I settled down in Forrest's tent, while Ma, Sarah May, and the girls got comfortable in the herder's shelter. I laid there for a long time listening to the distant voices of the men talking around a campfire. I hadn't realized I'd fallen asleep until I awoke to the soft patter of rain on the tent roof. Seemed Ma's weather forecasting wrist was never wrong.

Come sun-up it was another misty morning, but like the day before, by the time we had our wonderful breakfast in the wide outdoors it was all burned off.

As the women, Second Chance, and myself went back to our ramp patches, the men broke down camp and got everything ready to load on the horses and the mule. Once again Mary watched over the kids.

Around noon we all hauled our freshly harvested delicacies up to the edge of the meadow where they could be packed on our waiting equines.

197

With a bountiful haul, and a gaggle of rambunctious kids underfoot, we made our way down the mountain trail to the waiting wagons. There, the men hitched up the teams as heartfelt and joyous farewells were said all around. Then one by one, Pastor Wilson's buggy, the Grear and Fieldman wagons, and finally our own wagon pulled out and we began the long, slow journey to our homes.

It had been another exceptional ramp picnic.

FIFTEEN

U'thun'ta

I WAS JUST FINISHING my evening chores when Henry came strolling out of the forest.

"Thought you'd be ready to go," he said.

"As did I," I replied. "Would of been a bit quicker if you'd come and helped instead of watchin' from that gum tree over yonder."

Henry smiled. "Thought you said your pa wanted you to do your own chores. Woe be it that I come traipsin' in, causin' you trouble."

"Yeah, I hear ya," I smirked. "If it weren't for what Pa said, you'd o' rushed right in here and said, 'Billy, you sit yourself right down there and rest them poor feet of yourn. I'll take care of all them backbreakin' labors that you been afflicted with.'"

Henry laughed. "I'm a pretty good ol' boy, ain't I?"

199

I slugged him on the shoulder and said, "Come on, let's get my stuff and get goin'."

Pushin' and roughhousin', we ran to the kitchen where my bedroll sat next to a poke of venison jerky, corn dodgers, and four tallow candles. On the hand-hewn countertop by the dry sink sat a jug of sassafras tea.

Ma looked up from where she sat sewing a ripped sleeve on Pa's favorite work shirt.

"Why, hi there Henry," she said.

"Hello, Mrs. Banion," Henry said, coming to a sudden stop and standing real straight like he always did when addressing an elder.

"How's your Ma doing?" she asked.

"She's doin' good," Henry replied. "If she weren't, I'd've never left her overnight."

"Well, that's good," said Ma. "When you see her, tell her to come visiting if she gets a chance. I'd enjoy seein' her."

"I'll sure do that, Mrs. Banion," Henry said.

Ma then turned to me.

"Billy, come give me a kiss, and then you boys can run along. But you be careful now, ya hear?"

"Aw, Ma," I said, as I walked over and gave her a peck on the cheek. I then grabbed my things off the table and shouted, "See ya," before handing the clay jug to Henry and charging out the back door.

"Whoopee!" I heard Henry shout as we charged across the yard.

I laughed and whooped right back at him.

In no time, we stood gasping for air in the dusky confines of the chamber. On the sleeping shelf sat Henry's bedroll, which he'd dropped off on his way, along with a stack of brush and dried limbs for our campfire.

"You're all right," I said, eyeing the kindling.

"Yeah, a regular old Cherokee prince," he chuckled.

We both brushed off sleeping areas on the rock shelf with pine boughs, and then even spent a few minutes sweeping up the floor. Neither of us cared for the idea of stepping on scattered bones, or worse yet animal droppings, in the dead of the night.

After that, we laid out our bedrolls, snacks, and candles, along with two sturdy torches Henry had made from hardwood sticks and pitch-soaked pinecones. All that was left to do was to arrange the kindling for a campfire, leaving us with half an hour or so to explore the surrounding area before dark.

"On guard!" I cried, as I grabbed a switch and charged through the narrow passageway.

By twilight, as we re-entered the cave, we were boisterously joking and bragging about which of us had won the swashbuckling contest we'd fought. As you might imagine, there was no winner in that discussion. Truth be told, it didn't really matter. We were more interested in headin' for that jug of sassafras tea. We were parched beyond all reason, and Ma always did make some mighty fine tea. Henry then got out his flint and steel and sparked the fire to life. It always amazed me how he so expertly ignited birch fungus tinder with no more than a spark and a wisp of breath.

"You ain't figurin' on going back into that crawl, are ya?" I asked.

"Not this boy," said Henry. "I was thrilled to make it out alive the last time. Who can say what would happen if I tried it again?"

"Well, I'm glad to hear it," I said. "When I saw

that you'd made torches, I figured you might be fixin' to give it another go."

"No, them's for if we need to go out at night," he said. "Course, havin' candles, I don't reckon we'll be needin' em."

"I don't know," I said. "Torchlight seems more adventurous than candles. Let's keep em for when the fire burns out."

"Well, it's settled then," quipped Henry. "Torches for adventure, candles for comfort, and no exploring the mountain passage."

After a bit of thought he added, "But if it weren't for gettin' stuck, I sure would like to know where that passage goes."

We sat around talkin' and munchin' on jerky and corn dodgers while the fire glittered and glowed, sparks popping and snapping, sending flakes of glowing embers floating off into the darkness. After a while we got around to tellin' stories. Mostly just mishaps that happened around the Cove and long-winded tales about Black Gum Shoal. Then, of course, things graduated to more fitting, camping-in-a-cave, type ghost stories.

I started out with *The Legend of Sleepy Hollow*. Henry had never heard the tale before and got quite a kick out of it. We debated who and what the headless horseman was, and what had happened to Ichabod Crane after he encountered it. I figured he'd done been scared off and left the county, while Henry thought the horseman had got him. Whatever, we agreed he had it comin', the way he'd fetched after young Katrina Van Tassel the way he done.

Then Henry said he was gonna tell me about U'tlun'ta, or Spear Finger.

"U'tlun'ta," he said, "was a Cherokee witch-woman. She had skin and clothes that were rough and hard like rock. No arrows or other weapons could pierce her. It sounded like thunder when she walked because she crushed the hardest of stones and rocks under her bare feet. Her voice echoed through the mountains, scaring away the birds and wild animals of the forest, warnng of her forthcoming.

"She sang: 'Uwe la na tsiku. Su sa sai. Liver, I eat it. Su sa sai. Uwe la na tsiku. Su sa sai.'

"The forefinger of her right hand was long and sharp like a spear. Besides keeping it hidden in a fold

204

of her robe where no one would see it, she usually kept her hand folded because her heart, which was her only vulnerable spot, was in the center of her right palm.

"She was a shapeshifter who would often appear to the unwary as an old aunt from another village, or perhaps a grandmother or even a male member of the family. But she had to be cautious while in another form because she could not shift back if anyone was watching.

"Because of her treachery, many Cherokees were suspicious of anyone appearing from the forest alone. Were they the shapeshifter? It was safest to always be in pairs. If someone were to walk off into the forest, it may be Spear Finger disguised as them who returned.

"U'tlun'ta could stab a person in the back of the neck or in the heart with her long sharp spear finger and draw out their liver, which she would eat. The victim would show no visible wound, but within days they'd die. She'd often pull this trick on the sick or dying so no one would suspect her of killing them. But if someone offended her, she could take a healthy victim just as easily.

"If you looked at her closely, you'd see that her mouth was red from eating livers.

"She enjoyed appearing as a family member to lure children into the woods. She'd offer to comb their hair, or repair a torn dress, or maybe give them a juicy piece of fruit. But once that finger came out, the child was never seen again.

"As you might imagine, Cherokee younguns were taught from an early age not to stray into the woods alone.

"Spear Finger only had one enemy that she feared. He was called Stone Man.

"Stone Man was also a liver eater and shapeshifter. But he was even more powerful than she was. While she could stack up stones and melt them together to make bridges from mountain to mountain—what we today call stone archways, he could do using only his staff. He didn't even need to lift the stones. Also, instead of simply chasing animals away with his liver eatin' song, his low, grating voice could make the ground shake. What white men today call tremors.

"If Spear Finger had been away for a while, her

favorite way of finding Cherokee villages was to watch for smoke when they burned off hillsides to collect roasted chestnuts. She also looked for campfire smoke as it gathered in the valleys. If that didn't work, she'd simply wait by a stream for someone to come along and get a drink. Then, as light as the wind, she'd follow them home.

"It eventually got so bad that several villages united to try and find a way to kill U'tlun'ta. One of them had a wise old shaman who agreed to help."

"'First dig a great pit," he said. "Then cover it with limbs, leaves, and dirt.'"

"The villagers hurried out to do his bidding, then returned.

"Next, he said they should gather a great pile of green wood and burn it to make a towering cloud of smoke. This would draw the witch to them.

"They did that also."

"'Now we wait,'" he said.

"After some time, an old woman appeared from the forest pleading for help. She clutched at her cloak and wailed that Spear Finger was going to get her.

"Some of the warriors took pity on her and started

to go to her aid, but the shaman was not deceived. He stepped forward and threw his spear at her. The weapon flew true but shattered against her breast.

"The shape shifter, furious at having been discovered, screeched at the top of her lungs and pulled her spear-like finger from the folds of her cloak. Then, blinded by rage, she charged the warriors, unaware of the trap until it was too late. Down into the pit she plummeted.

"Eeya," she cried as she tried to change into a monstrous form. But with the people watching, she was stuck in the old woman disguise. She couldn't escape from the pit.

"Cheers arose as the Cherokees gathered 'round. Arrows flew and war clubs rained down upon the seemingly feeble woman. Yet, to the astonishment of all, no weapon could pierce her hide. Even her clothes showed no damage. She laughed as if being tickled. Her eyes flared with malice.

"Not even the shaman knew what to do.

"Then a titmouse bird known as Utsu'gi flew down and sang out, "un, un, un," which the Cherokees took to mean, "heart, heart, heart." They redirected their shots into her chest. The arrows shattered and the war clubs clattered to the ground.

"'Utsu'gi lies,' came the uproar.

"The warriors didn't realize they had misunderstood the faithful titmouse.

"Then, a chickadee, named Tsi'kilili, flew down and landed on U'tlun'ta's right hand.

"The warriors now understood. When U'tlun'ta raised her arm to drive the bird away, their greatest hunters fired as one, piercing her heart in the palm of her hand.

"U'tlun'ta cried out in shock and dismay, then slumped to the ground. Her reign of terror was over."

"Wow, I'm glad she's no longer around," I said.

"She may not be," said Henry, "but Stone Man still is."

"Well, why don't we ever hear about him?" I asked.

"They say, after Stone Man heard of U'tlun'ta's death and saw her spear fingered hand displayed at an Overhill village lodge, he took on the form of a Cherokee shaman and went to live alone in the mountains. Some say he is Two Hand," Henry added.

"Two Hand?" I gasped.

"Yes, Two Hand, the shapeshifter. He lives alone in

209

the mountains and legend says he's ageless. Where else could Stone Man have gone?" asked Henry.

"Well, I'll tell ya true. That 'bout gives me the heebie jeebies," I said. "Ya don't think he'd eat *our* livers, do ya?"

"No," replied Henry. "Ma thinks pretty highly of Two Hand. She says as long as he's in the mountains we have nothing to fear. In fact, if me and Ma travel any distance, or go somewhere at night, Two Hand shows up and walks with us."

"Wow, that must be creepy," I said.

"No, not really," said Henry. "He doesn't say much and leaves when we get where we're goin'."

"What's your Ma say about that?" I asked.

Henry shrugged. "She won't talk about it. Says I'm not supposed to talk about it either."

"Yeah, I know what ya mean," I said. "Pa's the same way about Two Hand. I don't know what it is they know, but I wish they'd let us in on it."

After a lively debate over who was the spookiest: Two Hand, Stone Man, or The Headless Horseman, we decided it was getting late, and called it a night. The fire was burning low, so we threw a few sticks on it and hit the sack.

210

SIXTEEN

Passage

THE SHELF WAS A great bed in theory, but not so much in practice. With a dank, midnight mist, slowly drifting down through the crack in the chamber ceiling, it was like trying to sleep on a coffin-sized ice cube. An involuntary shiver rippled down my spine making me curl into a tighter ball. I assumed it was my discomfort that had awakened me.

If only it had been so.

I shifted to find a more comfortable spot for my aching hip and stretched out my throbbing left arm.

"Don't move!" hissed Henry.

I laid still letting my sleep-crusted eyes scan the wavering light and shifting shadows in the chamber before me. A modest fire crackled and popped among the glittering embers on the floor. At some point Henry must have got up and added more fuel to the coals.

As I lay there, pondering my friend's hushed but harsh warning not to move, I noticed a strange object suspended above the flames. No, not one object I realized, but two. Yellow orbs floating about two feet off the ground. Something was in the cave with us. My sleep-muddled brain tried to register what I was seeing.

The orbs vanished, leaving a hole in the darkness, then just as quickly reappeared.

They weren't above the fire, I realized, but beyond it. Floating perhaps two feet off the ground.

"Stay real still," Henry whispered as he slowly reached down and retrieved one of his torches. "It's a panther."

A panther?!

With a practiced stealth that would have shamed a backwoods sprite, Henry stretched out his arm, touching the tip of his torch to the fire where its pine-tar-soaked cone flared to life.

At this, the floating orbs raised up several inches

in the dark and again blinked out and on.

Henry, silhouetted in the glow of flickering firelight, took a strong stance and slowly swept his weapon across the expanse between himself and the feline.

A low rumble drifted out of the darkness.

I couldn't help but picture an avenging King's Knight challenging his mortal enemy with a mighty, flaming, broad sword. Unfortunately, I suspect Henry had a somewhat different notion about the whole situation.

"Something's wrong with it," he muttered. "It should have run away when it realized it had been spotted. These things hunt by surprise. For it to stand and face a fire? I've never heard of such a thing."

He waved the torch back and forth as he took a small step forward.

The rumble transformed into a high-pitched hiss that rippled the short hairs on the back of my neck. A warning that echoed in the darkness as if the caverns very walls held a vendetta against us.

Henry stopped. Then took a hesitant step back.

"Get the candles," he uttered nearly inaudibly.

Sweeping my hands across the shelf behind me, not daring to take my eyes off the glowing points of terror beyond the fire, my fingers felt a bulge beneath the bedroll. Reaching under it, I withdrew all four candles.

"Got em," I whispered.

"Good," said Henry. "Give one to me, then light another off my torch."

I reached up and pressed one into Henry's outstretched hand while he kept eye contact, then lit a second off his torch as he'd requested.

While we were busy, the cat stood stock-still, though its eyes narrowed, and its snarl returned to a rumble. That was one mighty unhappy kitty, I can tell ya.

"Now, cross behind me and crawl into the passage," Henry said.

"What?" I blurted a bit louder than I meant to.

That brought on an angry barrage of snarling and hissing.

"We can't go in there," I muttered. "You nearly got stuck last time."

"We have no choice," declared Henry. "If it means

214

crawling through that tunnel or getting eaten by an angry panther, I'm crawling through the tunnel."

"But what if there's no way out?" I pled.

"If there's not, we'll wait for the panther to give up and go away," he said, "then come back out when it's safe to do so. I'm sure I saw a room back in there. And besides, I'm bigger than you are anyway. If I got turned around in there, so can you."

Of course, I was so flummoxed at the time, it never occurred to me that since Henry was bigger than me, if he got stuck *behind* me, I'd be stuck also. What good would turning around do me?

That's when the panther let loose with a full-throated snarl that sent me scampering for the passageway. Suddenly the prospects of what lay ahead seemed a lot less daunting than what laid behind.

I scrambled through the first part of the tunnel with no trouble at all. My only constraint was taking care not to accidentally extinguish the candle. Before I turned the bend, I paused to look back. In the soft, flickering light I could see Henry's outline twisting the torch handle into a craggy rock face to create a fire barrier between himself and the furious creature. A barrier that would only last as long as the pine-pitch torch burned; fifteen...maybe twenty minutes.

Henry then lit his candle off the torch flame and turned to follow me, the panther screeching in rage as it watched its prey getting away. Yet even its anger could not override its innate fear of the blazing pinecone before it. It hissed its hatred and scratched at the hard cave floor, powerless to pursue.

I turned to stare around the bend, peering into the stygian blackness. My weak candlelight revealed nothing more than a narrow, fissure-like passageway, much too small to crawl through on hands and knees. Tucking the remaining candles into the waist of my shirt, I stretched out on my right side and began squirming forward. Pulling with fingers and pushing with toes, trying to mimic what Henry had said he had done, I slowly crept forward. The flickering candle made progress difficult, but I sure wasn't of a mind to lose my only source of light to make advancing easier. If that candle had went out, I think I would have frozen up and died on the spot. How Henry had managed in the dark was beyond me.

After what seemed like hours, but could not have

been more than a few minutes, I reached the fissure into which Henry had forced his legs when he turned around. In the flickering light it seemed impossible. As he had said, he was slightly bigger than me, and I saw no way I could have fit my legs into that little crack. And he did it in the dark!

"Hurry up," I heard Henry utter from surprisingly close behind me. "That torch ain't gonna last forever." He gave my shoe a shove. "And I sure don't want that panther chewin' on my feet."

I squirmed past the cleft with a very unwelcome voice in my head bemoaning the fact that I was now in uncharted territory. I was farther along in the passage than Henry had gone before, and we had no idea what lay ahead: maybe the room Henry thought he'd seen, maybe an impassable blockage with no retreat, or maybe the crawl simply went on forever with no end. Even if the panther didn't get us, would we spend our last days slowly starving to death, our parents never knowing what had become of us?

I felt my heartbeat increase. I couldn't seem to get enough oxygen to breathe. I had an overwhelming urge to lash out and push aside the entire mountain that threatened to close in and crush me from existence.

"What's the hold-up?" urged Henry. "Let's go! Let's go! That torch is bound to be burning low."

Henry was right. There was no going back. I had to control my panic. Taking a deep breath, I steeled my nerves and concentrated on my breathing.

You can do this, Billy, I thought.

Pulling with my hands and kicking my feet, I advanced a couple more yards.

"Get on your knees," shouted Henry.

"What?" I stammered.

"I said get on your knees," he shouted again. "We hafta hurry."

I looked around in the dim light and realized the passage had widened out enough to flip over and crawl on my hands and knees. Odd that it took Henry's urging for me to notice.

With speed born of desperation, and hands burned from hot beeswax and melting tallow, I placed the butt of the candle in my mouth and forged ahead like an oversized mole invading a spring garden. The oily soot coated my nostrils and reddened my eyes, but I soon found I could pick up the pace. With the heels of my hands scraped, and the skin on my knees bruised, I forged ahead to outdistance the feline fiend.

Then my worst fears were realized. I came to a dead end. Just like that, the tunnel ended. A solid wall of dust-covered stone blocked my way. I had nowhere to go.

Henry bumped into me.

"What's the problem?" he asked.

"The tunnel petered out," I said unbelievingly. "It widened a bit, then just ended."

He raised his candle and looked around. "It can't just end," he said.

We sat there, soot faced and wide eyed.

"Now, what do we do?" I asked.

I could feel panic tryin' to take hold again. If not for Henry, I'm sure I'd have given in.

"I'm thinkin'," Henry said. "Before Pa died, he told me, 'Fear creates its own results. If you let it in, it will destroy you every time. If you don't, marvelous things may happen. After all, fear is nothing more than not knowing what is to come.

"'If a man was stranded on the side of a towering

cliff and lived to walk away, he has no fear because he knows the outcome. If he's still dangling, fear tries to take hold because he doesn't know what will be. It's best to remain calm and visualize a positive solution, then strive for that result. If you succeed, no fear was warranted. If you don't, at least you didn't let fear dictate your demise.'"

As he talked, he slowly moved his candle along the walls of our dungeon. Suddenly, the flame flickered.

"There!" he said. "Did you see that? There's a cross breeze. That means there's an exit here somewhere."

We both frantically scooted around, trying to find the source of the breeze.

"Over here," Henry muttered. "There's a hole in the ceiling."

I crawled over to where Henry was holding his candle up to an opening in the shelf above us. The sooty smoke that had burned our eyes drifted up into a crack about four feet long and perhaps a foot wide. Nothing but darkness laid above.

"It's not very big," I said. "Do you think we'll fit?"

"I'll try to shimmy through first," said Henry. "If I fit, we know you will."

"Okay," I said, not exactly happy with the arrangement. "But hurry, that panther may not be far behind us."

Henry raised his candle as far as possible then probed around with the handle of his unlit torch.

Until that moment I hadn't realized he'd managed to bring it with him.

When he was satisfied, he began squeezing into the overhead crevice. First his head disappeared, then his shoulders, and finally his chest. I could hear his shirt rip on the jagged rocks as he strained to push his slightly oversized body into the narrow opening.

"My head's out," he groaned. "There's a big room up here. I can't even see the walls or ceiling."

I watched him push with his legs but didn't see much movement. He slumped back down an inch or two and pushed again. This time he barely budged.

"What's the problem?" I asked.

At first, he didn't say anything; just kept slumping and pushing, slumping and pushing.

"What's wrong?" I repeated a bit louder, truly

getting worried.

I could see his calf muscles bunch below his trousers' legs. He pushed so hard it had to hurt.

"I think I'm stuck!" he finally said through clinched teeth and gasping breaths. "I can't move up or down."

"What'd you say?" I moaned.

I had heard him fine. Of course I'd heard him. I was right there, not three feet from his side. But there are times in a body's life when his mind refuses to acknowledge what it knows it heard. That was one of those times for me.

"I said I'm stuck!" he said louder.

Well, it didn't take long for me to realize that if he was stuck, so was I.

"You can't be stuck!" I admonished.

Silence filled the chamber.

After a moment he kicked his legs one more time, trying to find purchase. Still no luck.

"You can't be stuck," I repeated with the inkling of a whine in my voice that I hated. "That torch is bound to be burned out by now. How long do you think it'll take that cat to get here?"

"I know, I know," he said. "Just calm down."

After a minute of silence he said, "Okay, what I want you to do is reach up around me and see if you can find out what I'm caught on."

I nodded my head as if he could see me and scooted closer so I could stretch my arm into the opening. I felt all around. There were lots of jagged rocks and sharp edges, but I could find nothing that seemed to be holding him back.

"Nothing," I said. "You should be able to move."

"There has to be something," he declared. "I can't go up *or* down. Try again!"

Once more, I reached up and slid my hand along the rough walls of the tight passageway. I tugged on his shirt and searched for an impediment. Again, I came away empty handed.

"I'm going to try and push you through," I said.

Laying on my back on the cold cave floor, I placed both feet on his back side and pushed for all I was worth. All the while I was envisioning the panther charging through the tunnel.

"Ow, ow, ow!" he said. "Something's digging into my right shoulder blade."

223

I flipped over and jammed my hand up past his back. There was a knot of material gathered behind his shoulder. A rock had snagged the neck of his shirt as he was pushing up and got twisted in the material when he tried to lower himself back down. I guess, with as many sharp rocks as he had pressing into his back, he hadn't felt it.

"I found it!" I cried. "I found the snag. Hold on a second."

I prodded the bunched material several times with my fingertips, resistance prying back my nails. The discomfort was certainly noticeable, but I doubled my efforts, nonetheless.

Snap!

A pebble the size of a wild fox grape came cascading down into the corner of my right eye, but that was okay...the Knot gave way also!

I can't rightly say whether the tears on my cheek were due to the grit in my eyes or the flood of emotions that overwhelmed me, but I make no apologies either way. Salvation was at hand.

"You're free!" I called to Henry.

I needn't have bothered. As soon as he felt the

release of pressure off his shoulder, he shot through that hole like a greased pig through a split-rail fence.

But that ain't the amazing part. Lookin' back now; and don't fault me for the way I recall it, I believe I grabbed my candle, skittered right on past Henry, and was waiting up top when he came climbing through.

SEVENTEEN

Trapped

WE SAT IN A DIM circle of candlelight enjoying the fact that we were still both alive. Despite the coolness of the cavern air, we had both broken out into a heavy sweat and looked as if we'd been wallowing in Diver's new pigsty. Yet, on our faces were the biggest smiles you've ever seen—at least for a moment or two.

As if to challenge the very notion that we take the time to celebrate, a vicious snarl issued from the crevice we had just escaped from.

Henry snatched up his torch and quickly pressed his candle's flame to the sap-encrusted pinecone. Almost immediately a flickering blaze sputtered and popped to life; a blue and yellow flame encircled the conical head.

226

The panther, having already forced his gnashing muzzle and one front leg up through the crack, snarled and hissed at the pitiful light. Its eyes took on a fiendish yellow-red glow.

I jumped back as Henry thrust his flaming torch into the cat's face. With a painful screech, the beast tumbled into the cavern below. It would have chilled a grown man to hear the vented rage and fury in the very chamber that me and Henry had exited only moments before.

"Get some rocks," Henry cried, sweeping the torch back and forth along the gap. "Big ones!"

I immediately began groping around, looking for scattered stones. My tallow candle, not the strongest source of light in the best of circumstances, was but a spark of illumination in the vast cathedral of darkness. You'd be surprised how few rocks there are, lying about in a natural cavern. It's as if some great alluvial flood came along and carried them all away.

As I searched, I could hear the battle continue between Henry and the Beast . . . fang, against flame.

"Come on Billy!" Henry cried out. "This thing isn't giving up."

I redoubled my search, stumbling along, stooped low, the candle mere inches above the vast stone floor. Then, suddenly, I literally tumbled into a scattered pile of boulders. Some small, some large. They were everywhere. There must have been a cave-in in the distant pass leaving them there for me and Henry's use. And it was fortunate for us that there was.

"I found some," I hollered.

As I carefully swept the candle around looking for a good one, I realized I could not hold the candle and a rock at the same time. Finding a flat-topped stone too big for me to handle, I dripped some melting wax on the top of it and gently twisted the butt of my candle into it, securing it in place. Then, quickly stumbling among the boulders, I grabbed hold of a good-sized one. When I lifted, I like to broke my back. Letting go, I chose a smaller one. With a grunt and a groan, I managed to stand up and waddle toward Henry's torchlight.

"Watch out Henry," I said as I stumbled the last few feet.

Henry jumped back to let me drop the stone.

As it just so happened, the rock crashed into the waiting hole just as the enraged cat tried to thrust his savage head back through again.

I cringed at the sight and sound of the beast's face being smashed between the boulders. In the flickering light of Henry's torch, we saw its savage muzzle splattered with gore. Its upper lip was split open, and its nose gushed what appeared to be black liquid in the dusky light. In a small patch of sandy gravel near Henry's right foot, lay a fierce-looking, badly chipped canine. The cat's eyes were rolled up in its head and its tongue was hanging out of its mouth.

"Is it dead?" asked Henry.

"I don't know," I replied.

We both stood there, stunned at the sudden change of events. In an instant we had gone from possible prey to victors. We had faced down a demon of the forest and lived to tell about it. This was surely a feat to rank right up there with Hercules and the Hydra.

"YES!" I shouted. "Yes, we did it. Try to mess with us, will ya?"

Henry was smilin' a great big ol' goofy grin and

laughed right along with me.

"We're gonna be kings of the mountain tops," he said. "Whoopy!"

We were hoppin' around like a couple of dunce capped idiots.

Lookin' back, we're lucky we didn't break a leg.

"Ain't nobody gonna mess with us again," I gloated. "Why, if they even try . . ."

That's when the panther decided to come back to life. It wasn't a gradual reawakenin' neither. I'm tellin' ya that thing went from faint to fury quicker'n a bowl of spiked punch at an all-ladies social.

"Yow!" screamed Henry, jammin' the torch back into the hole.

The cat snarled and snapped its jaws, pullin' its damaged head back through the hole, leaving behind nothing but blood-smeared stones.

"Get more rocks!" screamed Henry. "Fast!"

I rushed back to my candle, grabbed another stone, carried it back to the hole, and gasping for breath, dropped it in.

Henry then handed me the torch and said, "I don't think it can get through, but keep it down anyway."

Several round trips and not a few smashed fingers later we sat down near the newly blocked crevice and caught our breath. Only holes much too small for the panther to squeeze through remained. We could still hear the snarling as he paced back and forth only feet below, but the combined weight of the rocks assured us that we were safe.

"I've never been so happy in my life for a stone-blocked passage," I said with relief. "Ain't a thing from here on out that could possibly make me fret."

In the quivering torchlight, I could see a bizarre caricature of Henry's dirt and sweat streaked face.

"Feel good, do ya?" he said.

I glanced back at the blocked passageway to reassure myself the panther could not escape its subterranean prison.

"Yeah, I feel great," I said. "Don't you? There's no way that cat can push his way through all that rock."

Henry hung his head for a moment, then looked me in the eye. "I hate to step on your celebration," he replied. "But if that cat's down there, and we're up here, how do we get home?"

I was dumbstruck. In all the excitement of tryin' not to get eaten, I hadn't even thought about how we were gonna get out of the cave. What if that passage was the only route.

I looked around at the absolute darkness of the cavernous underworld about us. The torch I held was no more than a tiny prick point of light in an endless expanse of night.

"What are we gonna do?" I whispered.

"I don't know, Billy. I just don't know," Henry said, as he placed both hands on top of his head and grasped his left wrist.

I'd often seen him do that when trying to work out a difficult problem. I sure hoped it helped.

"First off, let's put out that candle," he said.

"Put it out?" I questioned.

"Yeah, put it out," he repeated. "We need to save all the light we can."

Hurrying over, we snatched it up and blew it out.

"We hafta be careful with our light," Henry said. "You still have the other candles?"

I patted my shirt, and after a flash of panic, found both of them in a bulge of material at my back.

232

"Yeah, I've got 'em," I said.

"Good," Henry nodded. "That makes two whole candles, and two halves . . . assuming we can find the one I dropped when I lit the torch. Then we have the torch itself. How long ya figure a tallow-and-beeswax candle will burn? About six hours?"

"Yeah, thereabouts," I reckoned.

"I imagine we burned about two hours off the lit ones," he surmised. "That leaves maybe four hours each. So, with twelve hours on the whole ones, and eight on the stubs, that's what, twenty hours? With the torch about gone, that's what we got left if we only burn one at a time."

"But what if it goes out?" I asked.

He patted the pouch strapped around his neck.

"It won't be easy in the dark, but I reckon I got enough fungus tinder to light four or five candles," he said. "But we gotta get movin'."

The first thing we did was retrieve Henry's dropped stub. Then, while the torch still burned, we found a cave wall to follow. We had no idea which way to go, of course, but at least by following one wall we reasoned we wouldn't be walking in circles.

233

The torch gradually burned lower, giving less and less light, but we stumbled along in its weakened glow, not willing to part with it. We neither looked forward to following the wavering glow of a single candle. But, as we knew it would, time ran out. We lit a stub and stumbled along as best we could.

Henry led the way, candle in hand, while I grasped his ruined shirt from behind and stumbled along as best I could. Not that he would have left me, you understand, but in pitch-blackness the smallest separation feels like miles.

Here and there we had to veer around massive stalagmites or climb over collapsed mounds, but often the way was long and smooth like an underground hallway. Whichever, we always took great care to relocate our wall as soon as possible. It was the only guide we had to keep us traveling in a given direction.

Then Henry stopped.

"Do you hear that?" he asked.

"Hear what?" I whispered.

"Us," he said. "As we walk and breathe and scrape our feet. Before, it sounded hollow. Kinda like vanishing into the dark. Now it's different. I don't

234

know, it's hard to explain. It's like coming indoors from outside. The pitch of the sounds are different. I think the cave is gettin' smaller. The far wall is coming closer, and the ceiling is dropping too."

Before long we began seeing an occasional flicker of light reflect off the far wall. There was no longer any doubt. The chamber was shrinking. How Henry had sensed it I hadn't a clue. It all sounded the same to me. But it did somehow make me feel more secure. Not so exposed. Kinda like pulling a blanket up tight on a frosty night.

"How's the candle doin'?" I asked.

"It's gettin' low," Henry said. "I'm feelin' the heat."

He'd started with a partial candle rather than a whole one, so we hoped to get about four hours out of it. What we hadn't taken into consideration was, without a candle holder, it'll burn your hand before it goes out. We probably hadn't done better than three and a half hours.

"Feel around for a small, flat stone while you walk," Henry suggested. "Something we can use as a holder. That'll give us a bit more time."

"Good idea," I said.

I started kicking the floor of the cave with my shoe. I can tell ya, it didn't take but one or two stalagmites to

235

make me realize that wasn't the smartest move I'd ever made.

"Ouch!" I blurted as I hopped around trying to rub my bruised toe. "Forget it. Let's take a break. I'm tired. . . and thirsty too."

"Yeah, so am I," said Henry. "But let's go just a bit farther and see if we can find some water."

We walked, climbed, and scooted down slick mounds for another fifteen minutes or so before Henry came to a stop.

"I can't hold the candle any longer," he said. "It's too hot."

We hadn't found water, but we sat down anyway. Henry sat the meager stub on the cold floor as he built a small mound of fungus tinder. He then laid out his flint and steel along with a whole candle in preparation for continuing when our break was over.

"It's gonna be really dark when I blow this out," he said.

"Why not just let that little bit burn?" I asked.

"We can't Billy," he said. "We can't afford to waste any of it."

I knew he was right but didn't like the darkness.

"Here goes," he said. With that he blew it out.

236

EIGHTEEN

Revenge

PA AND DIVER, enjoying their after breakfast coffee, sat back from the table.

"Wonderful meal, Kate," Diver said. "Gives me strength for another day. Thank you."

Pa stood up and walked over behind Ma. He took her a bit by surprise when he put his arm around her waist and kissed her on the left ear.

"Yes, it was and does, Kathryn," he whispered. "I be thankin' ya as well."

Ma leaned back into him for a moment before shaking her head and straightening up.

"You two get on out of here and let me get my work done," she admonished. "I ain't got all day to be lollygaggin' around like some folks in these parts."

She wasn't foolin' anyone. With a bit of color on her cheeks and a twinkle in her eye, she gave Pa a flirtatious wink as she placed a water-filled dishpan on the dry sink.

From the way I heard it later, I don't reckon Mary had a thing on Ma.

Pa slapped Diver on the back and said, "Sounds like we got our marchin' orders, hoss. Oughta be a fine day by the looks of it. I figure by Thursday we'll have the plantin' done, then we'll see about that irrigation sluice box you been gagglin' about."

As they headed for the door, Ma cut in. "Oh, Zeb, on the way do you reckon you could check on them boys; make sure they're up and about? Tell em I'll have breakfast waitin'," she smiled. "That oughta hurry em along."

Pa grinned, "You ain't just flappin' your lips there. Ain't nothing'll motivate that boy like a bowl o' grits and a honey biscuit."

"Yeah, and I know just where he gets it from too," Ma said enjoying the lighthearted banter as she cleared the mornin' dishes off the table.

"How far ya say that cave is?" Pa asked Diver.

238

"Oh, it ain't but maybe ten minutes," he replied.

"Okay. Figure on em bein' a half hour or so," Pa said. "But don't be lettin' em sit around here all mornin' tellin' stories 'bout what a great adventure they had. There's chores to be done."

"Oh, get along now," Ma replied. "I know how to handle young uns."

Pa and Diver shooed chickens from underfoot as they crossed the yard and trudged over the bridge. They then turned east following the creek to the end of the pasture, climbed the fence, and entered the wood line as it skirted a steep hillside covered in rhododendrons.

Before long, Diver stopped and said, "This is it." He pulled aside a strand of greenery and showed Pa the entrance to the hidden chamber.

"Well, I'll be," Pa said. "No wonder I never saw it before. A person could pert near fall into it before noticin'."

They turned sideways to pass through the narrow crevice.

"Up and at it!" Pa bellowed into the murky light flowing from the crack in the ceiling above.

239

In the middle of the floor was a pile of glowing embers from last night's fire. Pa stepped around it and walked to the stone shelf at the back of the room.

"Come on boys. Time's a-waistin'," he called.

No movement. He reached down and patted one bedroll, then the other. Nothing. He threw em back.

"They're not here," he said.

Diver grabbed a fair-sized stick that was extending from the embers and used it to stir the fire back to life. As the room brightened, it became obvious the boys were nowhere to be found.

"Where'd them boys get to now?" asked Pa, more to himself than to Diver.

Pulling the now burning stick from the flame, Diver began a thorough search of the room. Pa, in the meantime, stepped outside and called for us. After several minutes he reentered the cave.

"Any luck?" he asked, not expecting an answer.

"I don't know," said Diver. "Come take a look at this." He stepped back so Pa could see the cramped passage at the end of the shelf.

"You don't think they'd a gone in there, do ya?" asked Pa.

"I don't know," replied Diver. "Where else could they be?"

"Billy!" Pa yelled into the cleft. "Are you in there? Billy! . . . Henry! . . . can you hear me?"

Pa and Diver knelt silently for a few moments and listened. "Billy! . . . Henry! . . . answer me!" Nothing.

Diver shrugged. "I doubt they're in there," he said. "Maybe they went home a different way, and we missed 'em. But why would they have left their stuff?"

"I don't know," said Pa. "Could be they were hopin' to spend another night."

"Maybe so," said Diver, grasping at straws. "Tell you what, you go back lookin' for 'em, and I'll stay here in case they show up. If Kate has any questions, it'd be best comin' from you."

Pa nodded. It was as good a plan as any. If the boys weren't there, Kathryn would immediately think the worst. He had flashes of the night they'd lost Weston; how it had nearly killed her. He just wasn't sure she could survive another loss.

Diver arose and stood next to Pa in the light of the fire. "I'll be right here," he assured him. "Things'll work out."

Pa nodded. "I'll be back as soon as I can."

Just as he turned to leave, a vicious snarl echoed through the stone-walled room. Both men jumped and spun around.

Like a nightmare exploding into real life, a large tawny panther came charging from the small passageway. It stopped in a crouched position, blood and spittle dripping from its muzzle. Its muscles bunched, and its claws scraped the stone floor. A snarl filled the chamber as its reddened chest heaved.

"Get back!" Pa warned as Diver stood frozen — dumbfounded.

The cat released its pent-up rage and leaped.

Most men would have died on that cavern floor, but Pa wasn't most men. With reflexes honed by years of wilderness life, and a youth spent fighting side by side with the likes of Two Hand, Jim Rainwater, and Davey Crockett, Pa spun and drove his iron-like fist into the beast's ribcage, propelling it over himself and out the vine-covered entrance way. When the cat crashed through the rhododendrons, it kept up its momentum and escaped into the waiting forest.

Diver regained his composure and hurried over to

Pa. "You okay?" he asked as he scanned Pa's face, arm, and shoulder for slash marks.

"Yeah, I don't think he got me," answered Pa. "But did you see his face? He was covered in blood."

Pa stood there unconsciously flexing his fists.

"I saw it," Diver reluctantly agreed. He walked over and examined the narrow entrance into the crawl. It was smeared with gore. "If they're in there, they may be hurt," he said. "I'm going in."

As Diver lowered himself onto his belly and probed the tight tunnel with his burning stick, Pa said, "Wait, he's my boy, I'll go."

Diver glanced up. "I'm not near your size, and I'm not sure that I'll fit." He shook his head. "Sorry, Zeb, it's gotta be me." He began crawling.

The first straight crawl was big enough for Diver's compact frame. He paused now and again to wipe blood from his hands but made good time to the bend. Then, looking down the vertical crack, he laid there aghast, there was no way! Us boys may have got through there, as did the cat, but there was no way a grown man was gonna do it.

"Billy!" he screamed. "Henry!" No answer.

243

Diver stayed there for ten minutes, calling and listening. Calling and listening. His makeshift torch had long since burned out, and the absolute darkness fostered little hope, yet he lingered all the same, not willing to accept the inevitable. Nothing existed down there other than silent eternal night.

Not being able to turn around, Diver finally began the long, arduous scoot back to fresh air. To sunlight. To freedom. To all the things he feared me and Henry would never know again.

Crawling out of that hole to face Pa without me and Henry in tow was the hardest thing he'd ever done. As his feet emerged, then his shoulders and finally his head, he saw Pa sitting in the corner of the stone chamber, head in hands. The weight of the world resting on his shoulders.

"What am I gonna tell Kathryn?" he mumbled in a weak voice.

Diver had no words. All he could do was silently support his friend as he grieved.

≈

"NO! . . . not my baby," Ma cried. "Not my Billy!"

Pa held her as she cried. He hugged her tight as she mindlessly beat at his back and sides. She pounded her forehead on his chest and left wet tear stains smudged on his shirt. Telling her what he and Diver had discovered like to have killed him. It was worse than bringing home the news about Weston. Weston had been ill; his passing wasn't unexpected.

Pa's mind went back to that terrible day. How he'd bundled the ailing baby, afflicted with milk sickness, in his great overcoat and trudged through miles of blowing snow, trying to get help. How the howling winds of a driving blizzard had tormented his every step. How he'd pushed himself through shifting drifts nearly as high as his waist and crossed frozen streams in winds so fierce they'd blown him hundreds of yards downstream before reaching the far bank. But through it all he'd persevered, never wavering in his struggle. He vaguely remembered coming to the home of Mable Davis, a local midwife and trusted healer. The searing pain in his nearly frozen fist as he pounded on her entryway in the wee hours of the morning. The welcoming glow of candlelight filling

245

the window and the screech of the opening door. And, finally, the trepidation he felt as he carefully handed her the frail infant only moments before collapsing on the cold wood floor.

Even with his Herculean efforts to save the child that night, it wasn't to be.

Though Ma recovered from the pneumonia she'd been suffering with, the loss was nearly too much. Pa watched as she sank into a deep depression that he feared would claim her life. A terror the family would come to call her 'low period' that left her bedridden for months. Even after she eventually regained her strength, she was lackluster and quiet. Only the birth of sweet Delma a full five years later restored her gusto for life.

That was all from the death of a sick baby, Pa thought. *How would she ever survive losing a healthy child? An unexpected tragedy.*

As Pa held Ma, he looked at Diver standing quietly at the end of the kitchen table with his hat in hand. His head was bowed, his face unashamedly streaked with tears.

"I need you to take the wagon and get Chance's

dogs," Pa said. "We've gotta stop that cat before it does this again." He gently turned Ma towards the bedroom. "And go by Forrest's place to tell him what happened. I could use Sarah May's help."

Diver nodded without saying a word and left the kitchen through the back door.

"I'm so sorry," Pa whispered into Ma's hair as he lowered his cheek to the top of her head. He knew she needed more comfort, but he was at a loss. For all his abilities, words of contentment had always eluded him. He simply repeated, "I'm so sorry."

Barely an hour after Diver had harnessed up the team, he came rattling back into the yard. The mules were sweat streaked and blowing hard while Chance's dogs pulled at their leashes in the bed of the wagon. Their baying carried across the woodlands in anticipation of the quest ahead.

Forrest and his family pulled in behind Diver, quickly climbing from their buggy and heading for the house.

While the Banions gathered around Ma's bed and listened to what Pa had to say, Diver unhitched the mules and Forrest's horse and led them into the corral where they could get water and feed. He then quickly brushed them down with a handful of straw.

Ten minutes later Pa and Forrest arrived, long guns in hand, and blood in their eyes. Diver couldn't help but note the similarities between the two statuesque men. A person would surely take them for brothers if they didn't know they were father and son.

"We ready here?" asked Pa.

"Let's do it," said Diver.

Pa and Forrest, each keeping a strong grasp on the excited dogs, followed Diver through the pasture and over the far rail fence. Crushing brush under foot, not willing to take the long way beside the stream, they soon arrived at the rhododendron cloaked cavern. Entering it, perhaps grasping at straws, they re-examined the chamber, hoping against hope for a missed clue that would suggest that all was not lost. Nothing was found. No one could have survived such a vicious creature in such a confined space as the crawl.

Tearing a leaf from the hanging vegetation, Pa smeared it with panther blood from the lip of the entranceway. He then held it up to Blue Boy's

248

sensitive nose.

"Find em boy!" he ordered.

He then did the same thing with Ricket.

The dogs could barely contain their excitement.

"Let's get at it," said Pa.

He led Blue Boy outside followed by Forrest and Ricket. The dogs immediately began sniffing the ground, racing back and forth . . . widening their search grid. In less than a minute, they had both zoned in on the spot where the panther had fled through the underbrush. They strained at their leashes barking in anticipation.

"Let 'em go," Pa said.

He and Forrest both slipped the leashes from the dog's collars.

In a leaf-shredding, twig-snapping rush, the powerful beasts lit out. Pa and the others slapped back limbs and sticker-bushes as they followed in pursuit. Scrapes and cuts were neither avoided, nor noticed. Killing the deadly panther was their only concern.

Pa normally delighted in the sound of baying hounds. It was music to his ears. But not on this day.

It simply enhanced the heat in his blood. Drove his thirst for revenge. Enticed him toward murder—if it were possible to murder a killer cat.

The chase continued for well over two hours. The dogs barking on occasion to alert their masters of their location. Then, with the hunt intensifying, and the scent growing hotter, they gave way to a full baying song. It was as if they were shouting, 'Hurry it up. It won't be long now.'

The men picked up the pace. An animal brought to ground didn't always stay that way.

Finally, the dogs overtook their prey. Cats have speed, but not endurance.

As the panther's heart slammed in its chest, quickly depleting the energy needed to flee, it first slowed, then stopped. Canines bared and claws extended, it turned to face its pursuers. Defiantly snarling and snapping, it slashed out at the very foliage about it.

Truth be told, few dogs can stand up to a fully grown panther with dangerous weaponry at every point: ripping teeth, slashing claws, and a lithe body that can swap ends at a moment's notice.

But Blue Boy and Ricket weren't just any dogs. They were in the death business. And they knew their business very well.

Immediately splitting up, they came at the cat from different directions. If it faced one, the other attacked from the rear. If it spun to face its tormenter, the first made it pay.

Outmaneuvered and unnerved, the feline quickly fled the stand-off and bolted up a nearby tree.

Though the dogs couldn't follow, they put up such a cacophony of noise the frightened cat stayed pat; grasping tightly to its perch, crouched low and snarling.

"They got him!" shouted Pa as he barreled down a steep mountainside to the valley floor below. His muscles were bunched like massive springs in an effort to maintain his speed. "It's treed!"

Forrest and Diver did the best they could to keep up. Neither had Pa's dexterity or innate drive.

After several minutes of following the rock-strewn canyon, they dropped off another slope and raced through a long-forgotten apple orchard bordered by a lush green mountain meadow awash with thousands

251

of wildflowers. Pa and Forrest didn't seem to take notice, but Diver was mesmerized. This was just the type of place he'd love to show me.

The thought crashed down on him like a mountain of sorrow. Never again would he show me the wonders of God's creation. Never again would he see the awe in my eyes. The pain was nearly beyond what he could bear. Yet he forced himself to follow his companions on their quest to rid the world of the demon that resided in a cat's hide.

At the far edge of the orchard, they came upon the site of the treed panther. It was hunched low on the large limb of a sycamore tree, hate-filled eyes glaring down at the leaping, barking, dogs. As the men drew near, the cat snarled and bunched its legs up under its body. Its tail twitched in apprehension.

"Surround the tree!" Pa hollered. "That panther's gonna jump!"

The men each took up positions around the tree cutting off all avenues of escape. Pa and Forrest checked their rifles. The cat mauled the limb, unleashing a shower of shredded bark.

"If you get the chance, go ahead and take the

shot," Pa encouraged Forrest.

"I don't have an opening," Forrest replied. "Too many branches on this side."

Being unarmed, Diver could do nothing but watch.

Pa raised his long gun and eased to the side. Sighting down the barrel, he relaxed, waiting for the panther to move. Mere inches would give him a clear shot between two branches if the cat but shifted its weight.

The panther fixated on Diver. Its eyes narrowed as its enraged brain chose him as the target of its fury. Hatred seethed through its veins as it tensed its powerful muscles. All else was forgotten . . . faded away as its glistening, golden eyes bored into the cause of its distress. It rose slightly, digging its claws into the limb. Spring-like tendons tightened to their apex. A soft hiss issued from its throat as it shifted forward, preparing to unleash its built-up energy.

Pa fired.

The .40 caliber ball ripped out the top of the cat's heart. It was dead before it hit the ground. Both dogs were on it at once.

"Back!" shouted Pa.

The dogs showed their superior training by immediately overcoming their natural tendencies to worry the beast. They backed away while all along keeping a sharp eye on the prey. A single sign of aggression would loose their restraint and draw them in for the kill.

The men stood looking at the sleek body. Each wrestling with his own thoughts and sorrows. It was Diver who finally drew his straight knife and said, "You two go on back to your families. I'll take care of this. Leave the dogs tied off over yonder."

Pa and Forrest silently put the leashes back on the dog's collars and tied them to a small pine tree. Father and son then turned and walked away, side by side, each with his head bowed, and his heart broken.

As they faded from sight, Diver knelt down and began skinning.

NINETEEN

Water Chute

HENRY YELLED, "CAREFUL!" as I slid down the smooth-rock water chute.

After taking a short break in the nerve-racking darkness, Henry had bent over his fire fixins, and holding a candle and frizzen in his left hand, used his right to make quick little strikes on his flint. Sparks showered down on the powdered fungus tinder until a small ember caught and slowly grew into a weak fire.

Quickly lowering his candle to the sputtering blaze, he miraculously managed to get the tip of the wick lit. Then, with an unseen smile on his lips, he tilted it downward so the small flame could grow into a usable light, an illusion of hope.

We'd had nothing to drink in several hours so after lightin' the candle, made that our number one

255

priority. Every hole and fissure in the stone floor were checked for dampness. Our ears listened for telltale sounds of dripping water. Even with the nerve-wracking knowledge of our likely doom if we didn't find a way out of that cavern soon, the thought of dying from thirst seemed to magnify the horrors. Then, far in the distance, we heard a hollow trickle. A tiny plop . . . plop . . . plop. A hushed voice of salvation creeping into our living nightmare. It was so soft we at first thought it was our imagination. But the plinking sound continued. It was real. It was out there. We just didn't know where. In the vastness of that lightless tomb, it was impossible to pinpoint the direction. All we knew was it wasn't behind us. So we continued in the direction we'd been going.

Amazingly, the sound grew. It went from a soft trickle to a definite splattering. It was water.

"Hurry," I said. "Don't worry about me, I'll be right behind ya."

Henry snorted and avowed, "I am hurryin'. Any faster and the candle's gonna blow out."

I shook my head as if he could see me in the darkness and said, "Well, don't do that. I'm just lettin' you know you don't need to wait on me. I'm so thirsty I could find that water by smell alone."

Within minutes we found it. More water than we could have hoped for. Wall to wall water.

Henry had to backtrack a step or two to find a place to sit the candle down. Then, more by feel than by the glow of the weak light, we both stretched out on the floor and lapped up the life-giving liquid.

"That's gotta be the best drink I've had in my whole life," I said.

It took Henry a moment to agree because his face was planted ear-deep in the stream.

After that we took a break, not knowing how long it would be before we found water again. We had no way of transporting it.

If we'd only known.

To continue, we had to step ankle-deep into the stream, which was wall to wall and gettin' deeper. Within an hour it was up to our waists.

"This isn't lookin' good," said Henry. "Gets much deeper and we're gonna hafta turn back."

"We can't," I said. "We've come too far."

I shivered and waited for his response, but it

257

didn't come.

Another half hour or so and the water had dropped to knee level. It still stretched from wall to wall but at least it didn't appear we'd be drowning any time soon.

By this time our eyes were about as light-sensitive as an eye can get. We still couldn't see any distance, but we could make out the walls and ceiling around us. We were in a tunnel-like passage, perhaps eight feet wide and ten to twelve feet high. Hundreds of stalactites, most small, but several large ones, sparkled above our heads. The watercourse we were walking in was, for the most part, smooth and level, yet when we came to a dip in the floor it tended to be quite slick.

My brain had somehow shut down the terror aspect of our predicament. I've since heard that's not uncommon. The body does what it can for self-preservation. I simply sloshed along in a dream-like state.

Then Henry stopped and said, "I need another candle."

I was dumbstruck. Reaching into my shirt, I

pulled out our final stick of tallow and bee's wax.

"It's the last one," I said.

"I know," said Henry. "After this we only have the stubs left."

That didn't bring a lot of comfort. I reluctantly placed the candle into Henry's waiting hand. After he lit it, I retrieved the stub and placed it into my shirt feeling the cooling wax stick to my clammy belly.

During the long hours of trudging through the sea of blackness, as I said, I'd forgotten what kinda predicament we were in. But when I handed that candle to Henry, our last candle, it all came crashing back. I think it was then that I lost hope. If not for Henry, I might have sat down right there in that freezing water and waited to die.

"Come on," said Henry, "it can't be far now."

How could Henry possibly know how much farther it was? Or even if the cave had an exit at all? How could he give assurances when he was as lost as I was?

Unwarranted anger swept over me. If Henry hadn't insisted we crawl through that passageway we wouldn't be in this fix.

A vision of the panther's blood-incrusted, snarling muzzle, flashed across my mind.

It wasn't Henry's fault we were in here. If anything, it was mine. I found the cave. I showed it to Henry. When he suggested we spend the night in it, I went along just to save face. It was almost like daring him to do it. How could Henry not blame *me* for the whole misadventure?

Suddenly it hit me. It wasn't Henry I was mad at; it was myself. It was because of me that my best friend would never see his Ma again. It was because of me that his body would be forever entombed in this dark underworld. It was all my fault.

"Hold on," Henry said, pulling me from my self-demeaning revelations. My mind cleared and I stepped up next to him.

"The floor's beginnin' to slope," he said. "The current's beginnin' to speed up."

I glanced down at the shadowy ripples around my lower legs.

"Yeah?" I prompted.

"It's like a water chute," he said. "You know, like the set of rapids below me and Ma's cabin. We're gonna have to sit down and ride it out."

"Are you nuts?" I burst. "We can't see!"

"I know," said Henry. "But what choice do we have? As long as there's no major drop-offs, and the ceiling doesn't dip too low, I think we'll be okay. Our main problem is, how do we keep the candle from going out?"

"We probably don't," I said, trying in vain to come up with a better alternative.

After a few moments, Henry pinched his sleeve.

"I've got an idea," he said. "Are your sleeves dry?"

We had been walking in shallow water for hours and our body heat had dried our upper clothing.

"Yeah, I think so," I said. "Why? You plannin' on settin' me ablaze?"

Henry laughed.

"No," he said. "I figure if we each rip a sleeve off, tie it in knots and bunch it up, we can light it on fire. Then holding the sleeve up in one hand, and a candle stub in the other, maybe we can slide to the bottom and light the stub before the sleeve goes out. Between us, we'll have two chances."

"Do you realize how crazy that sounds?" I asked.

261

"Actually, I do," he said. "But can you think of a better idea?"

I had to admit I couldn't. This was it. This was probably the end. I hoped Ma would be okay. I hoped she knew I loved her. Her and Pa too. And Diver.

Reaching up I grasped a ripped portion of my sleeve and pulled. It didn't give near as easily as I thought it would, but with a few tugs I managed to rip it loose. Then, reaching into my shirt, I removed the longest candle stub I had.

"I'm goin' first," I said.

"I can do it," said Henry.

"No, I got us into this and I'm goin' first. If I don't holler that I made it, perhaps you can find another way."

It was useless to argue about it. We were probably both dead anyway. Henry reluctantly relented and watched as I made my preparations.

Bunching my sleeve up, I sat in the cold water. Henry squeezed my shoulder and said, "Good luck." He then used his candle to light a knot in my ad-hoc linen torch. I immediately scooted forward and, almost without warning, was washed away.

"Careful," called Henry as I slid down the smooth, cold, water chute.

I can't say there was much carefulness to do with it. First thing I knew, I was flung from one wall of the chute to the other as it banked around a sharp curve. The next moment, water rushed up the outer wall like an inverted whirlpool sweeping me right along with it. I tumbled and tossed and felt my right shoe rip from my foot. The fire bundle and candle weren't even an afterthought as I lost both of them in mere seconds. In the absolute darkness it was impossible to tell up from down or side from side. My mouth filled with water as I tried to scream, and my shoe got tangled in my shirt. The next thing I remember was my back colliding with a huge rock. I must have spewed five gallons of water back into the stream. I was sure I was dead, but too busy to be scared. My feet caught onto something that sent me tumbling onto my stomach. I was suddenly sliding headfirst. Then I hit a series of drop-offs. I was on my back again, feet first in the water. I felt like a milk curd in Ma's butter churn. All hope was lost. Then I slammed into a large rock that stopped my momentum.

I groaned as I wrapped myself around that rock, rushing water pulling at my legs. All I could do was thank God that the tumbling had stopped. It took me several seconds to realize my arms and head were lyin' in a calm pool only inches deep. Reaching out, I pulled myself into the calmer water and found it sloped up onto a dry gravel bar. Coughing and spitting, I drug myself forward. Amazingly, I was still alive.

I was lost in a cave, far beneath a hard rock mountain, surrounded by a darkness beyond anything I could ever have imagined. But I was still alive.

I laid there, shivering and gagging. Coughing cold water from my sore, raw throat. Then, from far-off in that eternal night, I heard a voice.

"Billlly! . . . Billlly! Are you okaaay?"

It was Henry. He sounded hollow. And far, far, away. Kinda like an echo bouncing along a twisting and winding tunnel. I had survived but I was shocked that I could still hear his voice. I'd thought that water chute had taken me for miles and miles.

"Henry!" I shouted into the dark. "I'm here!"

I could hear my own voice echo along until it

faded to nothing.

A moment passed before I heard, "Are you alright?"

That actually brought a smile to my face. I was beat up, scraped up, bruised up, and half-drowned, but all in all I was okay.

"Yes!" I shouted back. "But I lost my light. The chute is too rough to hold onto anything."

Once again there was a pause, as if there was a time delay in receiving the message.

"I'm coming down," he shouted.

I thought about the rock that had stopped my progress. If not for that, there's no telling where I would have ended up.

"No!" I shouted back as quickly as possible. "Find another route. It's too dangerous!"

I laid there in the dark. Strangled yelps and cut-off gasps drawing near. Suddenly I was aware of Henry's coughing and gagging somewhere nearby.

"I'm here Henry!" I called. "Come toward my voice."

How he had gotten caught up on the same rock that had saved me from the torrent was nothing short

265

of a miracle.

I heard a deep-throated bout of retching, coughing, and spitting. Then gravel scraping. And finally, something touching my leg.

"Welcome, to the end of the trail," I said. "Ain't got much to offer ya, but come aboard all the same."

I heard some movement nearby as Henry crawled onto the gravel bar.

He then groaned.

"End of the trail is right," he said. "I lost my pouch. The flint and steel are gone."

I couldn't take any more bad news just then. My mind was overloaded.

"I'm tired, Henry," I said. "Let me sleep."

We both laid there in the darkness and let exhaustion overtake us.

TWENTY

Bad News

FORREST'S KIDS WERE STANDING by the pasture fence, petting and feeding the goat, when Pa and Forrest came walking out of the woods. They saw their father and rushed into his waiting arms. He hugged them tightly, thanking God for his blessings, and asking that he never has to goes through what his parents were enduring. First Weston as an infant, and now me, on the verge of manhood.

"I could just hug y'all to pieces," he said.

Looking at Pa, he saw the heart-wrenching pallor of his face.

"You kids run along now," he told his young'uns. "Grandpa and I have things to do."

Pa and Forrest continued toward the house.

"They're fine kids son," Pa managed. "You done

real good."

Forrest simply nodded and looked away as he rubbed his eyes. Pa was the strongest man he'd ever known, but some things just weren't bearable. To show as much fortitude as he was seemed miraculous.

As they drew near the house, Sarah May came out and stood on the front stoop. She wrung her hands in anxiety. The men's faces spoke volumes.

"She's sleeping," she said. "Got coffee on if you want some."

"Thank you, Sarah May," Pa said. "You don't know what it means to have you here right now."

He stood kinda lost for a moment, then cleared his throat and said, "I reckon, while Kathryn's sleepin', I oughta go tell Long Star what happened. I hate to do it, but it's gotta be done."

Forrest asked, "You want me to go with ya?"

Pa shook his head and patted Forrest on the shoulder. "No son," he said. "You stay here in case your ma needs ya. This is something I gotta do by myself."

As he turned to leave, Sarah May said, "Bring her back here with ya Pa. She shouldn't be alone at a time like this."

Pa nodded and said, "We'll be a couple hours."

Then, rifle in hand, he went to the barn to bridle and saddle his mules. With Pa's long-legged stride that burned miles at a pace that would near kill a man half his age, he didn't need to ride, but he knew Long Star wouldn't be up to walkin' on the way back.

Twenty minutes later, as he passed through a cane break on the lower fork of Black Gum Creek, Two Hand stepped from behind a boulder. He had a way of showing up when least expected.

"Zeb," he said. "What brings you to the real world? Getting too crowded in Tsiya'hi?" (Tsiya'hi, or Otter Place, was an ancient Cherokee name for the Cove.)

"Bad news," said Pa. He sat the butt of his flintlock on the pommel of Mac's saddle and let the barrel rest over his shoulder. He dreaded the thought of seeing the disappointment in Two Hand's eyes. He felt he'd failed in protecting us boys. Failed as a father, and a godfather.

"Our boys," he said, hanging his head and grasping his rifle so hard his knuckles whitened. "Our

269

boys are gone. Killed by a panther. Billy and Henry, both of them."

Two Hand's statuesque body appeared to slump a bit before quickly regaining its solid form. Pa once again conceded he must surely be standing in the presence of a living legend: a shaman, an ageless one, a shapeshifter. Perhaps even Stone Man himself. Surely no mere mortal could receive such news with such resolve.

"Tell me everything," Two Hand said.

Pa relayed the entire tale to him. From the camp-out in the cave, to finding us missing in the morning. From the appearance of the blood-covered panther to the hunt, and finally the kill.

When he was done, Two Hand nodded.

"Go home to your family. I will tell Long Star. We will come when she is ready."

With that, Pa handed Joleen's reins to Two Hand and silently turned toward home.

Early evening found Pa, Forrest, and Sarah May sitting around the kitchen table drinking yet another cup of coffee. Ma was once again fast asleep in her bedroom. Sleep was how she coped. Pa had seen it before. If it continued, she was headed toward a great depression from which she may never return.

"I don't know what to say to her," said Pa to no one in particular. "How to comfort her. If it were a man or beast, I could protect her. But this?"

"We know Pa," said Forrest.

Sarah May reached across the table and took his hands in hers. "It's in God's hands now. Trust in him."

Pa hung his head, unaccustomed to showing emotions. He knew Sarah May was right, but that brought little comfort. Then Diver walked in.

"Zeb, we need to talk," he said.

Pa knew Diver would never interrupt a family's time of sorrow without good reason. It wasn't in the man's nature.

"What is it, Diver?" he asked.

"I need you outside, if you don't mind," Diver said as he motioned toward the back door.

Rising, Pa followed Diver out back. The dogs sat panting in the yard as they walked to a nearby wall of fragrant mountain laurels. A cool breeze played softly among the blossoms. If not for the circumstances of the tragedy, it would have been a truly pleasant evening.

Pa stood as if defeated, waiting for Diver to speak.

"Sorry to interrupt, Zeb," he began. "But I didn't want to stir up what might be false hope without your say so."

"What are you talking about?" Pa asked. "What false hope?"

"Well, Zeb." Diver placed both hands on Pa's shoulders and tried to look into his downcast eyes. "I don't want you to get too excited cause I don't know exactly what this means, but I don't think that panther killed them boys."

Pa's head snapped up, bewildered. He anxiously repeated his last question, "What are you talking about?"

"When I started skinnin' out that panther, I noticed somethin' that seemed off to me," Diver stated. "Its face was torn up something fierce. Why should that be? Surely two boys couldn't have done that. At first, I racked it up to hopeful thinking. Not willing to accept the tragedy of it all. But when the hide was off, I got a closer look. That cat was not only

272

missin' a canine, but its gums were shredded, and its upper lip was plumb ripped in half. It even had a good section of its left ear hanging loose."

"Go on," said Pa.

"Now, I'm not sayin' them boys is okay, so don't be getting your hopes too high," said Diver, squeezing Pa's shoulders for emphasis. "But I am sayin', I don't think that panther got em."

Pa was dumbfounded. "But we saw the . . ." He couldn't finish the sentence.

"I know, Zeb," Diver said with a slight nod. "Just hear me out. Like I was sayin', as I was lookin' at all the damage on that panther's face it occurred to me that the blood we saw in the cave may not have come from the boys at all. It may have all come from the cat itself."

Pa stood there trying to grasp what Diver was telling him. Could it be? Could us boys truly be alive? Surely, this wasn't a cruel joke. Not from a man that loved me as if I was his own son.

"So," continued Diver, "I took a closer look at its teeth and claws. They didn't have a lick of fresh flesh on 'em. I'm sure you've taken plenty of prey animals after a fresh kill. Ever seen one that didn't have shreds of skin in their teeth and claws?"

Pa shook his head slowly and hesitantly as if he was in a dream state.

"So, I went a bit further," said Diver. "I cut open the cat's stomach. It was empty. That panther hadn't eaten in days."

"But that means?" Pa didn't really know what to think. "What you're sayin' is them boys are still out there! But where?"

"That I don't know," said Diver. "First thing I did was take the dogs back to the cave and checked it out again. I let 'em both get a good sniff of the bedrolls and sent Ricket into the crawl. She was probably in there a good thirty-five or forty minutes. When she came out, she seemed hyped up and ran around the room as if still searching. For what, I haven't a clue.

"I then sent Blue Boy in. Same thing. When he reappeared, the passage seemed to be of no interest to him.

"After that, I gave them another good sniff of the bedrolls and took 'em outside to see if they could pick up the scent. They ran around quite a while before

274

settling in on a trail that ended up bringing us right back here. I don't know where them boys got to, but I don't think that panther got them."

Pa stood there contemplating everything Diver had told him. If the cat hadn't got us, and we weren't in the cave, where were we?

"We need to get a search party together and find em," he said.

Looking at the failing light, he realized it was too late to start a search that evening. It would be dark within half an hour. He took a few quick steps to the back door and called for Forrest.

"Forrest, could you come on out here please?"

Following the scrape of chair legs on bare wood and hurried steps advancing across the kitchen floor, Forrest appeared in the doorway.

"Yeah, Pa?" he said.

"Forrest, Diver don't think that panther got Billy and Henry," Pa said. "And from what he told me, I agree. We don't know what happened to em, or where they got off to, but they're out there somewhere. It's too late to start a search tonight so we'll start in the morning. I need you and Diver to spread the word. I'd

275

go myself but your Ma may need me. Everyone willing to help is to meet here at first light. Tell em to be prepared to be out for a couple of days. Hopefully it won't take that long, but I'd rather they were prepared than not."

With that, Forrest went into the kitchen to inform Sarah May of what he'd be doin'. Diver and Pa got started on harnessing Mac and Forrest's horse and buggy. In no time they were ready to go.

"I'll take the east half of the Cove," said Forrest, "if you'll take the west."

"Let's do it," said Diver.

Forrest quickly flicked his reins and rattled out of the yard at a good trot.

"I can't thank you enough my friend," Pa said as he looked at Diver sitting on the tall mule. He reached out and patted Diver's knee. "I owe you so much."

"Nonsense," Diver said. "You know good and well I love that boy like he was my own. You don't owe me a thing."

Before Pa could say more, Diver tapped his heels on Mack's flanks and flicked the reins. He was grateful for the dusk. It hid the moisture in his eyes.

Pa went back inside to check on Ma. She was still sleeping, so he went out and milked Tilly while Sarah May prepared a light supper.

He couldn't shake his thoughts. Us boys could be hurt and in desperate need of help. Yet nothing could be done until sun-up. If they tried to search at night it would be fruitless. Might get someone else hurt or even killed. Could destroy sign too. Yet waiting sat wrong with Pa. He was a man of action. A man who faced challenges with unquestioning determination and grit. In his world, inaction was paramount to failure. And he refused to fail.

On the other hand, he knew blindly charging ahead was seldom the right course. This situation called for a carefully thought-out plan. The best action was usually the safest action. Wait for daylight and do this right.

He dropped his head accepting his limitations. In his many years of roaming the hills, whether hunting, trapping, fighting, or simply living off the land, he'd faced any number of wild beasts and dangerous foes. He'd weathered driving rain and piercing blizzards that would break most men. Yet he'd always come out on top. Everything that life threw at him, he'd met head-on.

But even Pa wasn't invincible. As he made his way back to the kitchen table and sat drinking lukewarm coffee, his heavy head slumped into his upturned hands. He seemed to be a defeated man.

Just after dark, a deep voice was heard from out front. "Zebulon, we have come."

It was Two Hand and Long Star.

Rising, Pa turned to Sarah May and said, "That'll be Long Star, Henry's mother. I'll send her in. Make her as comfortable as possible. She may not show it, but she's hurting just as much as we are. Two Hand will not enter. It's his way."

With that, Pa poured two cups of coffee and left the cabin.

"Long Star," he said. "I'm glad you came. I'm so sorry."

She stepped forward and hugged Pa but didn't say a word. Pa waited for her to step back and said, "Go into the kitchen. My daughter-in-law, Sarah May, is waiting to meet you. I need to talk with Two Hand for a moment."

278

Long Star nodded and went inside.

"Two Hand," Pa said as he handed him the cup of strong coffee. "We need to talk."

With that, Pa proceeded to fill him in on the new developments. How Diver had deduced that the blood may have all come from the panther itself. How its stomach was empty, and its teeth and claws were clean of fresh flesh. He then explained that there would be a search come first light with every man they could roust up in the Cove.

Two Hand listened intently, nodding from time to time, drinking coffee but showing no outward sign of emotion. He stood there as if unfazed, an ancient giant cut from stone.

When Pa had finished, Two Hand handed him back the empty cup.

"Your friend Diver is a good man," he said. "Tell Long Star all you have told me. She is strong. She should know the truth. I will go and spread the word among the Cherokee. From Tuckaleechee to Pointing Rock; from Black Gum Shoal to the Nantahala; we will search and drive toward this place. If the boys stand upon the Great One's earth, we will find them."

With that he gave Pa a firm arm shake and slipped into the growing dark.

Pa turned Joleen out into the corral and reentered the kitchen. The first thing he noticed was that Long Star wasn't there.

"Where'd she go?" he asked Sarah May.

Sarah, who was stooped over a pot of stew in the kitchen fireplace, looked over her shoulder and pointed a spoon at the bedroom door.

"Ma came out a few minutes ago and asked Long Star to come join her. I guess she feels they can comfort each other. I sent the kids up to Billy's room until suppers ready to keep them from underfoot."

Pa was taken aback, unsure of what to do.

"Reckon I should go in there?" he asked.

"No," Sarah May said. She placed the long wooden stirring spoon on the table. "I think it might be best to give them some mother-to-mother time."

Pa sat down. "Yeah, I reckon you're right," he said.

Another hour or so passed before they heard Forrest and Diver arrive out front. A few minutes later Forrest came in.

"Diver's puttin' up the stock, then he'll be in," Forrest said.

He headed for the fresh pot of coffee Sarah had made and poured himself a cup.

"We both made a pretty good circuit of the Cove," he said. "Everyone we talked to said they'll be here at first light. A few of them are still out spreadin' the word. I don't figure there'll be an able-bodied man within ten miles that's not here." He paused and sneered. "Except maybe Jud and Trace Beckett and their crew, that is."

"Ain't nothin' to be done about that," said Pa.

"It's hard to understand the pure mean in some folks," Sarah May said as she dished out the stew. "Them Becketts have about everything a body could ask for and yet they're just as spiteful as people can come. Now don't get me wrong. Orwell's a decent fella, even if he is the richest man in the county, but the rest of that bunch. Humpf!"

Pa had to smile. He'd never heard Sarah say a cross word about a single soul as long as he'd known her. He racked it up to tension.

Diver came in and said, "The animals are taken

care of."

Sarah May nodded and said, "Y'all sit down so I can feed ya."

She then stepped over to the ladder, and climbed part way up so she could see into the sleeping loft and speak without shouting, "You kids, come on down and get your supper."

A gang of tousle-headed kids were soon shuffling around trying to find a place at the table. Little Anny Lynn was quick to claim a prime spot on Pa's lap. When Sarah May went to move her, Pa shook his head. She let her be.

"Diver, would you mind giving the blessing?" asked Sarah May.

Diver lowered his head, and the rest followed suit.

"Heavenly Father, Lord of all creation, we humbly gather in Your presence and acknowledge You as our One Eternal Hope. We put our faith in You and know all things are for Your glory. We ask that these parents be reunited with their loved ones, trusting that nothing is beyond Your power. All things bow before You, and nothing can be but by Your Word. Place Your hand upon our hearts and guide us on our search tomorrow. Help us to bring those boys home. And we ask that You nourish our bodies and our minds with this wonderful meal Sarah May has prepared from Your bounty. In the name of Jesus Christ, our Lord and Savior, we pray. Amen.

Pa kissed Anny Lynn on top of her head. As the group of downcast men and frolicking kids began their meal, Sarah May fixed bowls for Ma and Long Star and took it to them.

After supper, Diver insisted Forrest and his family take his room in the barn while he slept by the fire in the kitchen. They objected to putting him out but relented to his assurance that he had a perfectly good reed mat that had served his needs just fine for many a long month.

Long Star used Billy's sleeping loft, and with Ma and Pa in their bedroom, everyone settled down to a long sleepless night.

TWENTY-ONE

Riches

CLARENCE TUDWELL, his sons Dean and Pat, and his son-in-law Rolf Schmidt, were the first to pull into Pa's yard the next morning. Pa greeted them as they climbed from their wagon.

"I appreciate this Clarence," he said, shaking the man's hand.

"No call to mention it Zeb," Clarence said. "It's what neighbors do. I just want to bring them boys home safe."

Diver watched the exchange from the barn where he had just finished milkin' Tilly and was gettin' ready for the goat. He nodded at the men approvingly as he repositioned the milk bucket to its best advantage.

"Them two are buildin' up a mighty strong bond," he informed the goat. She really didn't seem to care as she busied herself on a mouthful of flint corn. Diver smiled and washed her swollen udder.

A few minutes later, Chance pulled in with all nine of Orwell's farm hands resting on straw in a large freight wagon. Then came an assortment of farmers, craftsmen, and tradesmen, each lookin' to do their part. It was an impressive bunch including the Deerborn brothers, Percy Blyth and his son Roger, a classmate of mine, and even old Hester Wo. Wo was a cobbler by trade who worked by feel after going blind from drinking bad moonshine back in '72. What he was plannin' to do nobody knew, but the offer to help was appreciated.

Then came Thom Grear and his ranch hand Charley Wrightman. Charley was a mountain of a gal who could outwork and outfight just about every man in the Cove - and seemed to be on a mission to prove it. They brought along two wagons loaded down with Ben Cobb and all his neighbors who had witnessed what Diver had done for him.

Close behind the Grear Party came pastors Wilson and Steadman from the Cade's Cove Baptist and Methodist Churches followed by several male

285

members of their respective congregations.

It was an impressive turnout. Pa's heart swelled at seeing how many people were willing to sacrifice their time and energy to help "out-Covers", as Cove residents tended to call folks who lived in the surrounding mountains. It was hard enough to see after your own in them days.

"I'm mighty thankful to y'all for showin' up this mornin'," he said as the crowd gathered 'round. "As ya know, my boy Billy and his friend Henry Rainwater went missin' yesterday. At first, we thought a panther got em, but now we have reason to believe they got away. So, what's happened to em, we just don't know. It's not likely they got lost, so they may be hurt out there somewhere." He motioned toward the forested mountains. "I've sketched a map of the area where they were last seen. Everyone, take a look. Then get together with Forrest. He'll assign search grids. And like I said, you don't know how much I appreciate this."

Just as Pa was finishin' his brief speech, another wagon pulled up. It contained Jack Coleman and three of his co-workers. They all worked for either the

Beckett Mill or the Jud Beckett Freight Services.

Pa walked over and greeted the men as they climbed down from the heavy wagon.

"I'm surprised Jud let you men come up here," he said.

"We may work for the Becketts," Jack said as the others gathered 'round, "but we're our own men. If Jud wants to let us go for borrowin' one of his wagons and doin' the right thing, that's between him and his Maker. We'll survive. Where do you need us? We're here to find them boys."

Pa shook hands with each of them and told 'em to check with Forrest.

Diver had finished takin' the milk to the springhouse and sloppin' the pigs. He then met up with Pa. "Ready when you are," he said.

Pa hurried into the house to get his rifle and check on the women. Ma was once again asleep while Long Star kept busy helping Sarah May clean up after breakfast. Each coped in her own way.

"We're going now," he told Long Star. "Those boys gotta be out there somewhere. We ain't stoppin' 'till we find em."

"The Great One will guide you Zebulon," she said. "I will be waiting."

Forrest already knew where Pa and Diver would be searching. They wasted no time hitting the trail.

While the search party got under way, me and Henry laid there shivering in that damp, cold, seemingly endless cavern. I can't say how long we slept, but as for me, I felt as though I'd no more than closed my eyes before stirring again. Nothing but a prolonged blink, you might say. Yet, I reckon it must have been hours. My body ached, and my throat felt like I'd gargled with chicken feed. When I looked at Henry who was contently snoring flat on his back, my eyes seemed to be housing a whole nest of hungry termites.

I slowly, hesitantly, placed both elbows into the rough gravel under my sore back and digging in my heels, tried to shift my much-abused body to a more comfortable position. With a positively gallant effort,

I managed to scoot a few inches. Ahh, that was better.

Lying back, I rested my head on a long, narrow, somewhat brittle surface. Something snapped.

What was that? After an eternity surrounded by nothing but rock and water, it seemed out of place. It couldn't be natural. Could it?

I rubbed my head and then reached back to examine the strange object. It felt like a sack of sticks. That's when it struck me like a flash of lightning.

I SAW HENRY! HE WAS SNORING ON HIS BACK!

I glanced around. Near the far wall a swirling current shimmered where a weak ray of light fell on its surface. A bit nearer a small brown bat hung upside down by its self-locking talons. A drip of water sparkled as it dropped from a pencil-thin stalactite. How this could be, I hadn't a clue. Was it a dream? I closed my eyes.

"Please Lord, let it be," I whispered.

Bracing myself, I slowly reopened them. The light was dim, the surroundings hazy. But I could make out the arched passageway, the swiftly flowing water, and my best pal, Henry.

It was all real!

In the middle of the flowing deluge, I saw the towering rock that had stopped me and Henry's long swift ride down the chute allowing us to crawl onto the gravel bar. It stretched from floor to ceiling and appeared to be holding the weight of the entire mountain aloft. I couldn't have been more impressed if I'd seen Atlas himself standing there in that stream.

A hue of brilliance glimmered from around the column. Long beams of fading light dissipated in the darkness deeper in the cavern. A chill ran through my bones thinking about how close we'd come to being lost forever in that eternal void.

"Henry!" I shouted. "Henry. Wake up."

Henry's eyes snapped open. He sat up straight.

"What?" he growled, rubbing his lower back.

"Look around," I said with an uncontrollable grin. "Look around. There's light!"

Henry's head swiveled. There was a moment's pause. Slowly he rose to his feet, hunching his back to keep from hitting his head on the curved ceiling. He stared at the shimmering current.

"How?" he said, reaching out to touch a soft beam

of diffused light streaking past his face.

I smiled and pointed at the halo of brilliant light encircling the half-submerged column of rock.

"We must be near an exit," I said. "The way I figure it, it was dark when we passed out last night, so we couldn't see it. Now it's morning."

I flourished my hand like a master magician. "Voila!"

We cracked up. You'd be forgiven if you mistook us for a couple of dimwitted Yahoos straight outta *The Adventures of Gulliver*. We smiled and burst into laughter like lunatics. Hey, who could blame us? We'd lost our only source of light. Given up all hope of ever seeing our families again. Passed out, cold and hungry, from total exhaustion. We'd thought we were doomed to live out our last fleeting days lost and afraid in perpetual darkness. Even having fresh cold water to drink was a curse because it simply meant prolonging our agony until we starved to death. Then, to awaken with salvation at hand. Who wouldn't act like floppy-eared whelps seein' their first snowfall.

After leaping around a bit with excitement, my trodden-weary, half-frozen legs, buckled beneath me.

I sat down abruptly.

SNAP!

I'd landed on the sack of sticks I'd laid my head on earlier.

"What was that?" asked Henry.

"Oh, a sack of sticks I keep tangling with," I said.

I half stood and turned around to get a better look at the rotted, material wrapped bundle.

To my shock, it wasn't a sack of sticks at all. It was a partially crushed skeleton in what remained of old tattered buckskins. There was also a pair of cobbled shoes, the remnants of a Highlander's tam hat, and two brittle arrows dangling from holes in the buckskin shirt. A leather possibles bag laid nearby, and a badly rusted knife protruded from the ragged waistband of the leather breeches.

"Look at this," I said.

Henry shuffled over and looked at my discovery.

"Wow," he said, eyein' the eerie sight. "That could have been us."

That was one thought I could do without.

"Looks like he died of arrow wounds," Henry mused. "At least, he didn't starve to death while lost in a dark cave with no light."

I shuddered at the thought of it and said, "Yeah, at least not that."

As he knelt down next to the skeleton and reached for the decaying shirt, Henry said, "I wonder who he was. Maybe he has something on him that'll tell us."

He grasped the bottom edge of the shirt and lifted it up, exposing the knife. It was rusted almost beyond recognition. Only the handle, which looked to be made of some sort of shell or maybe a glassy rock, had survived the ravages of time. And even it was covered in a green fungus.

"I don't think we'll be gettin' anything off o' this," he said as he placed the knife in his shirt. "Let's see what's in the bag."

Reaching over, he gently tugged on the strap. It disintegrated. The bag's contents spilled across the cave floor. Dumbfounded, we both caught our breath as we stared. Scattered in the gravel at our feet were several strips of unknown material, a small awl, half a dozen lead musket balls, and more gold coins than most Cove folks had seen in their entire lives!

With shaky hands, Henry picked up one of the

coins. He flipped it in the air and caught it, testing its weight. He then vigorously rubbed it on his shirt before handing it to me and picking up another one.

"What ya reckon it is?" he asked.

I looked the coin over, marveling at its weight. As I raised it toward my eyes a beam of sunlight caught the freshly polished surface and flared. Even after all these years it hadn't lost its luster.

"Pa took me and Ma to Maryville once to visit with Delma," I said. "While we were there, a man brought one of these into her store. I remember, cause I'd never seen anything like it before. Ain't sense till now either. I think he called it a Spanish escudo. Pa said the heavier they are the more they're worth. This one feels mighty heavy to me."

It may seem odd but standin' there holding that coin I'd forgotten all about bein' cold. It's like that gold radiated heat plumb through my body.

"How many are there?" I asked Henry.

He scuttled over and picked 'em up one by one.

"Sixteen," he said.

I reckon Henry was holding more money in his hands right then than anybody I'd ever known. All except Orwell Beckett anyhow.

"We're rich," I uttered unbelievingly.

We both smiled.

Henry clutched the coins in both hands and said, "Let's get outta here."

Walking over to the column that supported the ceiling, I found a narrow passage tucked behind it with enough room to slip through. On the other side, bathed in sunlight, was a small ledge clinging to the mountainside. It couldn't have been more than ten feet by twenty. Skirting around the outer portion of the tower, I came to a hole in the cliff from which the water chute flowed. It plunged thirty-five or forty feet down a vertical fall, crashing among a tangle of massive boulders below. From there, a crystal stream meandered through a peaceful valley.

If I'd had any lunch to lose, I think I would have lost it right there. If either one of us had been swept past that column, our fate would have been sealed.

Henry soon appeared at my shoulder and stood contemplating the same site. A fortune rested in his hands while death played across his vision. As the sentiment goes — But for the grace of God.

Backing away from the falls, we first laid down our treasures, then looked around to take stock in our surroundings.

We were perched on a flat ledge perhaps forty feet up the side of a two-hundred-foot-deep canyon. The canyon was a good three hundred feet wide and had a similar vertical wall on the opposite side. The cliff face, both above and below us, was moss covered and slick from the constant mist rising from the falls. Beautiful sixty- and seventy-foot blue spruce trees dotted the landscape, but unfortunately, none closer than fifteen feet from our ledge. Much too far for us to jump.

"What do ya think?" Henry asked. "The skeleton back there obviously got up here somehow. I doubt he climbed with arrows stickin' out of him, and it's unlikely he came down that water chute the way we did. There must be another way up."

Loading our pockets with the gold coins, we began following the shelf around a prominence. On the other side we discovered a narrow ledge that seemed to lead down to the forest floor. It wasn't much more than a toe hold, and scary as all get-out, but unless we wanted to take up permanent residence with the eagles, we'd have to chance it.

"One wrong step and we'll reach solid ground before we planned to," I said.

Staring back and forth between the ledge and each other, we both stood there with nervous smiles on our faces.

"Nothing to it," said Henry.

"No, nothing at all," I agreed.

We both stood there, neither anxious to take the first step.

Finally, Henry said, "Well, this ain't gettin' us nowhere. Reckon I'll scoot on out there."

To my shock and surprise, I heard myself say, "No, I'll do it. You led the way through the cave, I'll lead the way down to the valley floor."

Henry seemed to think about that for a moment before relenting.

I'd have preferred an argument.

With nothing more to say, I faced the cliff and stretched out both arms as far as I could, feeling for divots to hold on to. Then, shuffling my feet sideways, I began to inch across the wall.

"Careful," Henry said as I rounded a bulge. "I'm right behind you."

It was a terrifying feeling, hanging out there on that narrow ledge some thirty-five feet or so above the canyon floor. I kept my right cheek planted firmly against the cold stone wall fearing if I turned my head I'd plummet backwards. Every few minutes I'd stop, close my eyes, and let my heart rate settle. I'd then continue, advancing mostly by feel alone. I soon got into a rhythm. Move left hand, find grip, move left foot. Move right hand, find grip, move right foot. Take break, deep breath, repeat. My confidence was growing.

Suddenly, there was no ledge beneath my left foot. My body began to pull away from the wall. I desperately grasped as hard as I could with my fingertips. By the grace of God, I resettled.

Heart pounding, I cautiously glanced down beneath my left arm. Nearly ten feet of ledge was missing. It must have collapsed sometime in the distant past. Wouldn't you know it! Ten whole feet gone. And, that ten feet may as well have been a mile. With the narrow foothold we had, we sure couldn't jump it. As I studied on it, it became abundantly clear. There was no way across. We were flat out stuck . . . again!

Heavy hearted, I carefully looked back at Henry.

"Go back," I said. "The ledge ends. There's no way down."

The sentiment I'd relayed to Henry in the cave came echoing back. "Welcome to the end of the trail."

Henry, to his credit, didn't ask any questions. He simply turned back and retraced his way to the shelf.

With nothing else to do as we sat in the glorious, early morning sun. A sight we'd given up all hope of seeing mere hours before. Henry pulled out the rusty knife and began polishing its handle with his shirttail.

I pulled out a coin and spitting on it, rubbed it between my fingers. It was stamped with the image of a big nosed man on its face. I had no idea who he was, but I was sure glad to make his acquaintance. If only we lived long enough to introduce him around.

"Who you reckon that skeleton in there is?" I asked Henry, nodding toward the cave.

Henry didn't answer right off. He was still workin' on the knife handle.

"Reckon he must have been awful important, having all this money," I said. "Maybe he was a pirate. You think a pirate might have come all the way up here from the coast?"

Henry shrugged. "If he stole the captain's gold and they were chasing him, he might have," he said.

"Then he ran into the wrong bunch of Indians and all that gold didn't do him a lick of good anyway." I mused. "What a pity."

Henry finished polishing the knife handle and looked at it closely. He spat on it, rubbed a bit more, then looked again.

"I don't think it was no pirate," he said.

"Why not?" I asked. "It's as good a story as any."

Henry held out the old glassy handle and said, "Take a look."

I stared at it for a few moments, seeing nothing but scratches. Then it became clear: MZ.

Moss Zeekman!

My heart flipped in my chest.

TWENTY-TWO

Tudwell's Trouble

D IVER DODGED YET another branch as he followed Pa through a rather thick stretch of overgrown sticker-bushes. Pa had been setting a steady pace all morning and Diver had to admit he wasn't sure if he could keep it up much longer. To his relief, they came to a small stream where Pa called for a break. Though hating to slow Pa down, and figuring the respite was for his benefit, he appreciated it.

The valley they had been sweeping was six miles long and over half a mile wide. It lay between the cave and Henry's home on Black Gum Shoal.

Henry, of course, knew the mountains between

Black Gum Shoal and the Cove like the back of his own hand. But in the dark, especially while running from a panther, anybody might get turned around— even Henry. Then, if something went wrong; a broken leg or a thorn through the instep, well, we may not have been willing to split up. Perhaps settled into a safe place and waited for help to come along.

I figure that was his reasoning anyway.

Three times they'd traversed the tangled width of the valley in hopes of cutting our trail. So far with no luck.

As they sat there, catching their breath on the stream bank, Pa snapped off a twig and began idly scratching at a patch of mud between his feet. He glanced over at Diver and sorta cleared his throat. He appeared to have somethin' to say, but didn't quite know how to bring the subject up. Finally, he stilled himself and just came out with it.

"You really believe that stuff you said at supper last night?"

"What's that?" asked Diver.

"Well, ya know, about God being all powerful, and Him being our only hope, and all that?"

302

"Yes, Zeb, I truly believe it," said Diver. "I believe He's all powerful, all forgiving, and all loving. I believe He's our Creator, our salvation, and our only hope."

"So, how's a body get all that hope?" Pa asked.

"Ain't a physical thing a person can do," said Diver. "Jesus done did it when He died for all mankind. Why, He took every sin there ever was and ever will be upon Himself. Can you imagine that? Just flat out cleaned the slate. He done it as a gift. Nothing we can do to deserve it; we just gotta eccept it. Just ask for forgiveness, and believe it's been given. Ain't nothing but a matter of faith."

"Yeah, that's the way I understood it was supposed to work," Pa said. "But to tell ya the truth, I been mighty bitter ever since little Weston died. Seein' Kathryn go through what she did. Reckon I kinda blamed God for it. If He is so lovin' and all, why do bad things happen to good folks."

"I understand what you're sayin', Zeb," Diver replied. "And it ain't always easy knowin' why things happen the way they do. But I'll tell ya this much. He does have a plan, and I reckon He knows what He's doin'. We just have to have a little faith. He'll see us

303

through."

"Well, I'm asking ya to a be a witness right now," said Pa. "I'm asking God to give us back our boys. Not for me, but for Kathryn and Long Star. Two of the finest women that ever walked this earth. And I pledge right now, if He does that, I'll change my ways. I ain't sayin' I'll never fail. I ain't that strong a man. But I'm saying I'll give it my best."

With that, Pa stood up and continued the search.

"Why don't I stay with the stream and keep an eye on the banks?" suggested Diver. "If they're lost in this mess, surely they'll need water. I don't think they'd leave it."

"Good idea," said Pa. "I'll check out the higher ground and meet you at the abandoned Indian village at the head of the valley. You can't miss it. It's where this no-name stream meets Abrams Creek."

Pa nodded to Diver before turning back into the twisted brush. Twigs snapped and displaced leaves showered to the ground as he disappeared from sight. Diver diligently worked his way upstream toward the abandoned village.

In the meantime, Clarence and his boys worked

their way down his west property line, past Orwell's holdings, and into the broken country north of Abrams Creek. It didn't seem likely we'd have gone that way, but all them canyons needed to be checked anyhow. If they could, they'd meet up with Pa and Diver at the old Indian village on Abram's Creek. By design, their search grid wasn't anywhere near as long as Pa's, but it was much steeper.

Me and Henry had no idea we'd triggered such a massive search. We figured Diver would've found us missing and surmised went into the crawl (which we did) and got stuck or lost (which we also did). And since they couldn't reach us, they'd have no choice but to mourn us and go on with life. I sure did hate Ma not knowin' what happened to me.

"You ever wondered what life would be like without you?" I asked Henry.

We were sittin' on the edge of the cliff watchin' squirrels and wrens carry on a bloodless battle in the spruce trees. The wrens were protecting their eggs, and the squirrels were protecting their babies. As far as we could tell, neither side was really interested in stealing from the other, but both acted like they were being threatened anyway.

"No, can't say that I have," said Henry.

We sat in silence for a bit longer, then Henry tapped my knee and pointed.

"Look at that," he said.

I followed his finger and saw a pair of river otters bounding out of the stream down the falls. Water cascaded off their silky pelts as they raced up the grassy bank. Reaching the top, they dropped to their bellies and used the slope as a slide. Slicing into the shimmering current, they soon reappeared and did barrel rolls before repeating the whole process again.

"Looks like fun," I said. "They made a water slide but they ain't got nothin' on us."

Henry laughed. "You got that right. Why, I reckon we're about the biggest kings of the water slide there's ever been?"

"King Henry," I said.

"And King William," came his reply.

It's kinda hard to figure how two boys that had been through what we had, and who were still trapped on a ledge, could sit there and joke with each other. I reckon it's true what they say about the resilience of youth.

≈

By mid-afternoon, Diver reached the old village. He hadn't picked up any sign of our passing but held out hope that we were nearby. Needin' something to do while waiting on Pa, he decided to light a large, smoky, greenwood fire as a guide. Just in case we could see it.

Then he sat on the banks of Abrams Creek and speared a few trout. They'd brought provisions for a couple of days, but fresh fish was always welcome.

In the meantime, Pa climbed every pinnacle he could find that might give him a sight advantage. He scoured the hillsides and the valley with seemingly boundless energy. He was a man obsessed. A father in search of his son.

≈

On the western slope of the opposite ridge from Pa, Clarence was trying hard to prevent his own son from plunging to his death off a shifting embankment.

Knowing the terrain of their search area, they had brought plenty of rope. Fortunately, Pat, Clarence's youngest son, had tied off before trying to cross a large scree field on a steep hillside.

With a single wrap around a wind-swept cedar tree, Clarence had let out the safety line as Pat eased his way across. Then, without warning, the entire hillside gave way. Pat scrambled and clutched at shifting stones, trying in vain to find purchase on the moving mass. It was to no avail. Pebble-sized rocks and man-sized boulders all traveled together over the precipice and crashed into the valley below. Pat, by hopping and dodging, managed to avoid most of the larger obstacles, but soon disappeared over the edge himself.

Clarence only had time to get one quick wrap of

the rope around his forearm before his son's full weight hit him.

"Dean," he shouted as the rope shredded his flesh. Furrows burned into his hands. In desperation, he planted one foot behind a boulder, grabbed the tail of the rope, and flung it around his leg to create a second friction point to stop the slippage. Even so, several feet of rope slipped through his sweat and dust-caked grip, burning and abrading his leg. Blood flowed freely before the line finally came to a stop.

At his yell, both Dean and Rolf, who were working their way through a stand of pines farther up the ridge, reacted instantly. They rushed out of the treeline and hurried to their father's aid. Dean grabbed the rope to take pressure off his father's leg while Rolf straddled the tree and began pulling Pat from the abyss. Muscles strained and lungs heaved. The rope inched upward.

"You okay, Pa?" Dean asked his father as he gasped for breath.

Clarence just waved and motioned for Dean to go help Rolf.

Within moments Pat's head emerged over the

rim. As they pulled, they could see he was wide-eyed and straining to get a handhold on anything that wasn't moving. He seemed to be a might bit excited and not overly happy about his present situation. It may have tickled the boys some if it hadn't given em the willies. A few more tugs and they had him sitting on a solid slab of sandstone well above the scree field.

"Don't think I'd've taken that route," said Dean.

Pat looked up still tryin' to catch his breath. He smiled and said, "Now you tell me."

Dean slapped Pat on the back. Not hard. Just enough to say, "Don't ever do that again."

Rolf was looking at Clarence's hands.

"They'll be alright," said Clarence trying to shake some of the sting out of em. At best it did nothing but fling some blood around.

Rolf ripped long strips of cloth from his shirt and began wrapping his father-in-law's hands.

"Yeah, I reckon they'll mend," he said. He then pulled up Clarence's pant leg to see the torn and bloody flesh beneath. "But I'm afraid your hunt is over."

Taking off the rest of his shirt, he began working

on the gaping wound.

"We gotta find them boys," Clarence said.

"We'll find em," said Rolf. "But first, we gotta get you off this mountain. The shape you're in, you'll just slow us down."

He stood looking around. "We can't take ya back over the ridge, so I reckon we'll follow the edge of that cliff yonder and hopefully work our way down and back to the wagon. Pat can take you home while me and Dean will continue the search."

As they scanned the canyon lip they saw smoke drifting across the late afternoon sky. "Wonder what that is?" Rolf said more to himself than to anybody else.

"Hope it don't rain tonight," said Henry.

I looked up at the long streaks of scattered white clouds in the light-blue sky. Just beyond a far-off ridgeline a blush of orange-red tint was beginning to paint the horizon.

"I'm with you," I said. "We could always go back in the cave, but I ain't hankerin' to ever do that again."

Henry just nodded, looking off into the distance.

"What you reckon that is?"

I followed his gaze out over the far wall. There, in the distance, was a smudge of grey-black smoke. As we watched, it grew into a charcoal-like column before catching in the wind and drifting away.

"It's a fire," I said. "A campfire. And it looks like it's just beyond that hill."

We were thrilled that someone was so close. But could we get their attention?

We shouted and screamed and carried on until we were blue in the face. The wild creatures of the valley scattered and disappeared. Even the birds abandoned their nests and flew over the nearest ridge. Of course it was all to no avail. No one that far away could hear us down in our canyon. Especially with a ridge in between us. But just the idea that someone was just beyond the next hill gave us hope. We sat back and happily talked about all the things we were gonna do when we got down from there.

≈

Unbeknownst to us, Dean, Pat, and Rolf were having quite a time tryin' to get Clarence off that mountain. His hands looked like he'd taken a rat-tail file to 'em. Not all that unusual for a cattleman. Just an inconvenience. Rope burns were a part of life. Even with shredded palms and throbbing fingers, he'd make do.

The real problem was his leg. It was swollen to about half again its natural size and was hurtin' him something fierce. He couldn't bear the slightest pressure on it. Even his pant leg was insufferable. He'd been through plenty of scrapes and bruises in his life, but nothing like this. If it hadn't been for his boys being there, he'd have flat-out shown the world that a grown man really can cry.

"Hang in there, Pa," said Dean. "This ledge is clear plumb down to the bottom. We'll have you off here in no time."

All the young men were exhausted from trying to

get their Pa off the mountain with as little stress on his leg as possible. They had studied the heavily wooded terrain they'd face descending the mountain slope and concluded the only passable route was within ten feet or so from the edge of a canyon. There was a narrow, rock-strewn path, mostly devoid of brush and trees.

With one boy beneath each arm and the third clearing obstacles out of the way, they carefully worked their way down the precipice. Each shelf-rock was tested to be sure it wouldn't break loose and take them over the edge.

Clarence wasn't a small man to start with and just may have put on additional bulk over the previous winter.

A fact his boys could attest to.

And half-carrying such a man down that tract of loose rock alongside a hundred-foot drop-off was both heart-stopping and backbreaking work. Every ten minutes or so the boys would swap positions to give their arms a break before continuing the slow pace.

"I sure hate this," said Clarence. "Putting y'all through all this."

Pat was just gettin' settled in under Clarence's left arm.

"Now don't you be startin' in on nothin' like that, Pa," he said. "If it weren't for you doing what you done, I'd've been snatchin' air all the way to the canyon floor."

As Pat was talkin', and Dean and Rolf were gettin' repositioned, Clarence thought he saw movement about halfway down the far wall.

"Hold on a minute," he said, grasping both Dean and Pat by the shoulder for support. He leaned back, where he could see around a tree and down into the canyon below.

"Well, I'll be," he said. "Will ya take a look at that. I done found them boys."

TWENTY-THREE

Who's First

PAT, DEAN, AND ROLF looked over the lip of the cliff as their Pa had indicated. To their shock and amazement, they saw about the last thing any of them would have expected. There, on a shelf of rock about halfway down the opposite wall of the canyon, sat me and Henry. We appeared to be lollygaggin' and whatnot next to a beautiful free-flowing waterfall like we were on a Sunday picnic without a care in the world.

Leaving Clarence in Pat and Rolf's capable hands, Dean stepped into full sight of our ledge. He placed his hands on each side of his mouth and hollered out in a strong voice.

"Hello down there!"

We both jumped up and looked around. Across the way, we spotted the Tudwells callin' and vigorously wavin' their arms from atop the far canyon wall. They were maybe fifty feet higher than us, and framed out just right to see between the treetops. Any higher or lower on the bluff and the view would have been blocked by the towering pines. I've often marveled at how fortunate it was that Clarence saw us right when he did.

As they stood there waving, me and Henry waved right back at 'em. That was a mighty fine moment. I can tell ya that.

Clarence, standin' on one leg and keepin' a hand firmly planted on Pat's shoulder, placed his other hand upside his mouth and hollered, "Are you boys alright?"

I hollered right back, "We're mighty hungry, but fit as a fiddle."

"Can you get down from there?" he shouted.

Shaking my head, I yelled, "No! The way down collapsed. We're stuck."

"Okay," he called. I saw him reach back and grab Rolf's arm with his free hand. He seemed to be havin' trouble standing on his feet. "Just hang in there. We'll get ya down."

Clarence then had his boys help him find a comfortable place to sit while still being able to see us.

"Okay, Rolf," he said, "I want you to take the ropes and see if you can get down there where them boys are. If so, see if there's a way to get em off that cliff."

He then turned to Pat and Dean.

"I want you two to go find whoever built that campfire. It may be Zeb and Diver over at that old Indian village where we was plannin' on meetin' 'em. Tell em we found the boys and bring em back down yonder. I'll be fine where I am, so get to it."

Understanding the urgency of the situation, the boys set out on their tasks.

Rolf, shouldering the ropes, followed the canyon wall to its base, crossed the stream, and retraced his steps back to the waterfall. When he saw our predicament, and how the ledge had given way, he agreed it was impassable. Walking about, he studied the situation but found no ready solution.

Henry and I just sat there with our legs dangling, trusting somebody would find a way to get us down.

In the meantime, Pat and Dean were wasting no

time racing to find help. At first, they sacrificed a bit of skin from their hands and shins by forcing their way through thorn-baring brambles. But reaching the perpetual shade beneath the Fraser fir and red spruce forest, the underbrush cleared and greatly speeded up their progress. The only problem with that, was they could no longer see the smoke. They had to continue by dead reckoning alone. Luckily, they came across Abrams Creek and followed it to the camp. There they saw Diver spitting a fish over a fire.

"Hello the camp!" shouted Dean as they rushed into the sunlight.

"Hello yourself," echoed Diver.

"We found 'em!" yelled Pat. "We found them boys."

Diver's legs nearly buckled.

"You found 'em?" He sputtered unbelievingly.

"That's right," said Dean, "and they're alright."

"What's going on?" came a yell from afar.

Diver and the brothers turned to see Pa rushing up the middle of no-name stream. Water splashed from bank to bank and his rifle thrust fore and aft as he plowed through like a buffalo in tallgrass.

"What's happening?" he shouted.

"Found 'em!" Diver called back. He pointed at Pat and Dean. "They found Billy and Henry!"

As Pa made his way across Abrams Creek and clasped Diver's hand to help him up the bank, Dean and Pat were about falling over each other trying to spout out the good news.

"We found 'em, Mister Banion," cried Pat.

"Both of them," said Dean.

"And they claim to be just fine."

"They're okay?" repeated Pa. "They ain't hurt none?"

"They say they ain't hurt any," said Dean. "Course we ain't actually looked 'em over any, cause when we left to get ya they were still stuck up there."

"Stuck up where?" asked Pa.

"Stuck up...? Well, come on," said Pat, "We'll show ya."

In less than twenty minutes of jumping deadfalls and pushing through clinging evergreen boughs, they came to the hidden entrance of a steep-walled box canyon. A crystal-clear stream cascaded over age-smoothed boulders in its midst. Without breaking

320

stride they turned into the shaded valley, leaping from rock to rock, and clamoring over moss-covered logs. Soon they saw Rolf Schmitt standing at the base of a crashing waterfall.

"Mighty glad to see ya, Mister Banion," he said.

"Where's my boys?" asked Pa.

Rolf smiled and pointed up.

Pa looked up to see me and Henry peeking over the edge of our rocky prison.

"Howdy, Pa," I shouted. "Diver."

Pa and Diver both looked worn to a frazzle.

"You boys alright?" Pa called.

"Yeah, we ain't hurt none," I answered. "But we sure could use a bite to eat."

"Okay, just hang in there. We'll get ya down."

Pa looked around noticing Clarence was missin'. "Where's your Pa?" he asked Dean.

"Up yonder," Dean said, pointing to the top of the far canyon wall. "He done got injured and can't get down on his own."

"Hurt bad, is he?" Pa asked.

"Tore up his leg pretty good," said Dean. "Too painful to walk on by himself."

Pa looked at the steep slope. "Can you boys get him down from there okay?" he asked.

"Yeah, we done got him halfway down," Dean said. "He had us leave him where he's at after we saw Billy and Henry so's we could go find you."

"Okay," said Pa. "I appreciate it. Y'all go ahead and take care of him. Me and Diver will get the boys down."

Turning to Rolf he said, "I'd be thankin' ya for the use of that rope you got there."

"Sure thing, Mister Banion," said Rolf as he took the rope off his shoulder and handed it to Pa.

With that, the Tudwells started back downstream while Pa and Diver looked the situation over.

"What d'ya think?" asked Pa.

"Well, I'm thinkin' I could climb that big pine yonder and throw a rope over to em," he said. "Once they tie it off, I could shimmy across and lower em down."

Pa looked at the towering pine and the distance from cliff to tree.

"That's gonna be an iffy shimmy," he said. "A man falls from that height, he ain't gettin' back up any time soon."

He scratched his chin.

"Reckon I better be the one to do it."

"Yeah, I figured you'd be sayin' that," said Diver. "But look at it this way. I'm a might bit lighter than you are. Them thin limbs on that tree up there are gonna be tested even with *my* weight. No reason makin' things more dangerous than they hafta be."

Pa didn't like it, but he knew Diver was right. It just wasn't easy puttin' someone else at risk when it was his job to do.

"Okay," he uttered. "But you be real careful. Any doubts at all, you come back down, and we'll find another way."

Diver patted Pa on the arm and took the rope. He placed it over his head and let it rest on his left shoulder.

"Ain't looking to be no hero," he said. "Just tryin' to get them boys home. If it feels too risky, I promise I'll come back down and we'll build a ladder."

Pa nodded and helped Diver get into the lower branches. Within minutes, he had to back off in order to see his progress. It was quite a performance. If he didn't know better, he'd say Diver clambered up trees every mornin' just for the grins of it. Kinda made Pa smile a bit. For perhaps the hundredth time, he wondered where that man had come from.

While Pa watched Diver from the ground, me and Henry did the same from our ledge. Nobody said a word, not wanting to distract him while he climbed. Within minutes, he was at our level.

"Howdy boys," he said. "Y'all think you might could use a little help?"

"Oh, we're just hangin' 'round watchin' the day go by," I said. "But seein's how you're here anyway, and it feels like it might be gettin' on to suppertime, I don't reckon we'd make too big a fuss if you were to get us down from here."

Diver laughed and said, "Got somethin' for ya."

He threw over a leather poke.

Pickin' it up, we looked inside. Corn dodgers and elk jerky. Yes! Even if we weren't bein' rescued, we'd a been as happy as pollywogs in a mud puddle right about then. We started gammin' meat and bread into our mouths like chipmunks under a wind-blown hickory tree.

"Y'all think one of you could take the time to catch this rope," called Diver. "Tie it off on something so I can get outta this tree."

Henry, his cheeks too stuffed to speak, sputtered, "Thure." He then stretched out his hands.

It took three tries, but we finally caught it. Two wraps around a big rock near the cave entrance, and a double square knot, and we felt it was secure.

"That oughta do it," I called.

Diver pulled the slack tight and fastened his end to the tree with a slip knot. He then tucked the extra length into his waistband and carefully eased his weight down on the drooping span.

Hand over hand, knee over knee, he worked his way across the divide. The rope dipped, and the tree swayed, but with infinite care, he made it to the rough rock wall. A few tugs and kicks, and maybe a grunt here or there, found him sprawled out on his back, gulping air and glad to be on solid ground.

"Welcome to our abode," I said, smiling down at the spent man.

Tearing off yet another piece of elk jerky, I stuffed it into my mouth.

Truth be told, I never was a big fan of elk meat. Too gamey. Even compared with deep woods boar. But right about then, that elk was some of the finest jerky I ever tasted.

Diver nodded. "Give me a minute," he said. "Let me catch my breath."

After a bit, he sat up and pulled the rope from where he'd tucked it in his pants. A tug or two released it from the tree.

"Good man!" called Pa.

We all looked at Pa's upturned face. My heart flipped once more. It sure was a long way down there.

"Reckon I can lower y'all from here," Diver said, lookin' at me and Henry. "Who's first?"

Good old Henry manned right up, sayin', "He is!" All the while pointin' at me with a big ol' grin on his face.

Diver laughed. "Good for you Billy," he said. "I'm proud of ya. Always jumpin' right in no matter the risk. If only to save a friend from peril."

He winked at Henry.

I stood dumbfounded. What could I say? I couldn't hardly argue the point. Not after Diver piled praise on me. Even if it was in jest.

I had to clear my throat before sayin', "I guess I'm first."

I wasn't as cordial with Henry as Diver had been. I squeezed my nose, furled my brows, and gave him a "skunk-in-the-outhouse-stink-eye". He knew the implications. A "skunk house stink eye" was even worse than a double dog dare ya. You couldn't take it back till the deed was repaid.

Diver rigged the rope in such a way that I could sit on it, hold it in my hands, and have it tied around my waist, all at the same time. He called it a 'bosun's chair', though in all truth, there wasn't any chair to it.

With one wrap of the rope around the anchor rock, to help control my descent, he had me slip over the edge.

I can tell ya true. I was happy to be goin' home, but givin' up the safety of that ledge didn't tickle me a bit.

As Diver and Henry played out the line, I more or less walked my way down the wall. It was an odd sensation, danglin' in mid-air while ya shuffle down a cliff face backwards. Between you and me, I ain't

327

hankerin' to do it again.

Next came Henry.

"Ain't nothin' to it," I hollered. "That rope held me, it oughta hold you."

Henry gave a dismissive scoff, but I noticed his shoulders tense.

I have to admit, I covered my mouth and smiled.

Diver then climbed down himself.

Pa, as you can imagine, was over the moon that he was taking us home. He hugged us both, then held us out at arm's length to make sure we weren't injured. He then hugged us again.

I'd never seen that part of the man before.

After that, he threatened to tan our hides if we ever put him and Ma through such an ordeal again.

All in all, it was a pretty fine reunion.

By the time we made it back to Abrams Creek, Clarence and his boys were just coming off the last of the slope. They met us at the confluence of the streams. There, we all had another grand reunion. Pa nearly beatin' poor Clarence half to death thankin' him for finding me and Henry.

After that, against Clarence's wishes, Pa ordered

Dean and Pat to help him get Clarence onto his back. He carried that man all the way to his wagon. It took forty-five minutes, and Pa made it look like he was carrying no more than a basket of eggs.

When we got to the wagon, everyone made a fuss over makin' sure Clarence was comfortable enough. He kept sayin' he was, but no one seemed to be payin' him no mind. It got so bad he finally threw his hands in the air and shouted, "Get your cotton-pickin' hands off of me! I ain't no papoose to be bundled up and pampered."

That got everyone so tickled that even Clarence got to chucklin'. Between the oohs and aahs of his painful wounds, that is.

All in all, we had a real good time on our way home.

Dean dropped me, Pa, Henry and Diver off at the base of the Cove trail. It was agreed all around there was no reason to be jostlin' Clarence up that old track. The man had a tough enough row ahead of him.

After a last round of heartfelt thanks and fond farewells, we set our sights for home. We were dirty, tired, ragged, and hungry . . . and four of the happiest chaps you'd ever wanna meet.

I couldn't have been more proud than to walk that hill with the finest men I've ever known.

"I'm comin' home Ma," I murmured.

Epilogue

NOW DON'T BE FRETTIN' NONE, cause I got a whole heap a stories to be tellin' ya yet. It's just that sittin' around on the porch like this is gettin' mighty taxing on this old man's backside, if you know what I'm sayin'. Sides that, I hear the wife in there grumblin' 'bout me sittin' out here just a-jawin' rather than gettin' my chores done. Truth be told, I ain't never got overly fond of doin' chores if I got somethin' better to do.

Anyway, y'all be sure and come back, cause I ain't half done tellin' ya's 'bout them days of my boyhood in the Cove. 'Bout Ma and Pa, Henry and Long Star, the old shapeshifter, Two Hand, sweet Mary Wilson, Second Chance, Tyrone, and all the rest. But most of all, I wanna tell ya Diver's story. And how he was God's own blessing to our Home In The Mist.